THE ALAMO

A NEWMARKET PICTORIAL MOVIEBOOK

THE ALAMO

The Illustrated Story of the Epic Film

Text by Frank Thompson

NEWMARKET PRESS
New York

This book is published in the United States of America.

First Edition

10 9 8 7 6 5 4 3 2 1
1-55704-606-9 (Paperback)

10 9 8 7 6 5 4 3 2 1
1-55704-607-7 (Hardcover)

Library of Congress Cataloging-in-Publication Data available upon request.

QUANTITY PURCHASES
Companies, professional groups, clubs, and other organizations may qualify for special terms when ordering quantities of this title. For information, write Special Sales Department, Newmarket Press, 18 East 48th Street, New York, NY 10017; call (212) 832-3575; fax (212) 832-3629; or e-mail mailbox@newmarketpress.com.

www.newmarketpress.com

Designed by Deborah Daly

MANUFACTURED IN THE UNITED STATES OF AMERICA.

CONTENTS

FOREWORD
John Lee Hancock

Over the past year and some odd months many people have asked me how I got involved with the making of the motion picture *The Alamo*. As I think about it now there are myriad possible "correct" answers.

The genesis of my involvement may have been when Ron Howard asked me to read a draft of the screenplay and give my opinion of the movie he was, at that time, going to direct. My many story conversations with Ron deepened my respect for him and provided valuable insight into his filmic intentions regarding *The Alamo*.

It may have been when Ron withdrew as director, remaining on as producer (with Mark Johnson and Brian Grazer). It was then that Dick Cook, Chairman of Walt Disney Studios, asked me if I had any interest in rewriting and directing the movie. For the record I answered that I was "intrigued."

Or perhaps it went back further, to a BBQ hosted by Joe and Sharon Ely some six years ago outside of Austin. At this event, held on the weekend of the Austin Screenwriters Conference, I listened in on a discussion between screenwriters Leslie Bohem and Randall Wallace. The topic was Davy Crockett. Their opinions on the man ranged from the mythic—Randy is, after all, from Tennessee—to the historical. By the end of the conversation, Les had decided that he wanted to write a screenplay about the siege of the Alamo based on current historical knowledge.

Or maybe my involvement with *The Alamo* started a long time ago, back to a summer vacation when I was eight years old. My family lived in Texas City, Texas, and every year we went to San Antonio to visit my grandmother. This particular year Mom and Dad decided a field trip was in order. We packed sandwiches and drove the station wagon downtown. After walking past banks and hotels I first laid eyes on the structure which has since and forever haunted and thrilled me—the Alamo church.

I'd like to report that I remember every second of that excursion, every step taken on the site, every glimpse of every artifact of historical significance. I can't.

What I do remember is feeling very small inside the church and being awed by the reverence extended the place by visitors; their whispers echoing in the room sounded to me supernatural, as if they were conversing with the souls of the people who had died there. I felt it in my bones that something important had occurred in this place. I also remember that the thick stone walls were very cold against my back.

So, I suppose, the answer to the question of how this all started for me could be any or all of the above. No one answer. No one truth. Memories are like that. History is like that.

Alan Huffines begins his book *Blood of Noble Men* with a Mexican proverb. It reads: "History is a cruel trick played on the dead by the living." I've come to hold this quote dear and to recognize that each of us who attempts to tell the story of the Alamo, whether in words or images, is doomed to some degree of failure. Seemingly every source one finds defends itself against a counter source; every bit of data carries an asterisk that puts its relevance or veracity in question.

During pre-production I began working with several fine historians who helped me detail incidents from the Texian, Tejano, and Mexican points of view. They were all invaluable in helping make sense of the complexities of the time, place, and ramifications of this event in history. Armed with all this information I should have been prepared to shoot the movie, and yet I had a nagging suspicion that I was missing something.

I brought up my predicament with Michael Corenblith, our talented production designer, who wisely reminded me that in any true story there exists both a factual and emotional truth. And that, to be faithful to the tale, you need a balance of both. His words struck a chord. I had concentrated so hard on the historical data that I had forgotten the emotion of the story.

Much has been made of the fact that I am a Texan directing the most important of Texas stories—as though my heritage gives me a leg up on understanding the relevant history. It doesn't. Anyone with a library card and a few months of down time can learn as much or more than I have. So what do I know?

I know that in the Alamo whispers conjure the spirits of the men and women who came before.

I know that something unique and important happened within the walls of that lonely old church.

And I know that the thick stone walls are cold against your back.

HISTORY
IN THE MAKING
THE FILMING OF *The Alamo*

It is bitterly cold in the bleak hours before dawn on March 6. Beyond the walls of the Alamo, hundreds of Mexican soldiers huddle on the wet grass, shivering in the night air. They wait anxiously and silently for the order which will propel them toward the old mission-turned fort, toward glory—or disaster. They have drilled for this day week after grueling week. They have fired rifle and cannon shot at the Alamo. And now, the time has come. They scarcely breathe, listening for the word that will begin an event of matchless courage and a nightmare of slaughter and horror. And then it comes…

"Action!"

When the attack is over—or, at least, the portion of the attack filmed that night—the cast and crew of *The Alamo* gather to pay homage to the real men who fought and died exactly 167 years ago tonight.

Screenwriter/director John Lee Hancock remembers, "We had thirteen seconds of silence for all the men who had died there on that day. It was a quiet, solemn moment."

He continues, "We had been filming the assault on the north wall and I thought, 'Here we are in the heart of the assault on the day it happened.' It had already become a scary thing, just being at night. The approach was always to go from absolute silence to the cacophony of sounds and flares and cannon and musket fire and noise of battle. That terror was something that we had kept in our mind when we were planning it—to not make it just a battle, but more like a nightmare. I remember it being especially creepy and sad, especially when we wrapped, and the sun's coming up…. But during those thirteen seconds, I looked around a little bit, and not a person was moving. I think it affected a lot of people there."

* * *

[Above right] Cinematographer Dean Semler (left) lines up a shot while director John Lee Hancock (second from right) looks on. [Right] John Lee Hancock and Dennis Quaid prepare for a scene at the battle of San Jacinto.

The battle of the Alamo has been fought in the movies and on television over twenty times, dating back to 1911. Its story of heroism and sacrifice has proven irresistible to filmmakers and audiences and has attracted stars such as John Wayne, Fess Parker, Glenn Ford, James Arness, Raul Julia, Joel McCrea, Ernest Borgnine, Alec Baldwin and numerous others.

The last major big screen *The Alamo* was John Wayne's epic version, filmed in 1959 and released the following year. Because of its bigger-than-life telling of the saga of the Alamo (not to mention its bigger-than-life star/producer/director John Wayne), *The Alamo* has become an authentic classic of the American cinema, beloved by millions of fans—and even, against their better judgment—many historians.

But despite the affection in which Wayne's *The Alamo* is held, it was a "Hollywood movie" in all that that implies. The characters and events were fictionalized and the settings created for maximum cinematic impact, not for authenticity. Like all Alamo movies that preceded it—and most that followed it—*The Alamo* was a complete work of fiction.

But throughout the 1990s there was a new wave of Alamo scholarship. Historians were digging up new information, solving riddles, challenging long-held beliefs, asking new questions. The Alamo began to be seen less as a legendary story of a tiny band of good Americans overwhelmed by an army of bad Mexicans and more as a complex issue in which both sides had legitimate points of view.

Some of these new histories of the Alamo were controversial, and the authors found themselves under siege by the true believers in the Alamo myth. Issues such as whether Travis actually drew his famous "line in the sand," or the precise nature of the death of David Crockett, could—and still can—easily rouse anger. Dan Kilgore, author of a little book called *How Did Davy Die?*, actually received death threats for suggesting that Crockett might have surrendered and been executed after the battle.

"WHEN I FIRST GOT HERE AND I WALKED ON THIS SET, I GOT A CHILL UP MY BACK-BONE LIKE I CAN'T DESCRIBE. IT HELPED US THROUGHOUT THIS WHOLE MOVIE. AND EVERY TIME WE WALKED THROUGH THE GATE OVER THERE, WE WERE IN THE ALAMO, YOU KNOW? I DON'T MEAN TO SOUND PRETENTIOUS ABOUT THAT. IT'S JUST THE TRUTH."
—Billy Bob Thornton (David Crockett)

For screenwriter Leslie Bohem, the new wave in Alamo scholarship inspired an idea that the time was right to make another Alamo film—a film based on fact, not patriotic fancy.

"I grew up on the Alamo," says Bohem. "It was always one of my favorite stories. Over the years, I knew from the movies of my youth and the books I read back then that they weren't getting the whole story, which is so wonderfully rich and complicated."

Bohem and executive producer Todd Hallowell took the project to Academy Award®-winning director Ron Howard, who became enthusiastic about Bohem's idea of telling the true story of the Alamo. Howard brought production designer Michael Corenblith on board. Corenblith had received two Academy Award nominations on previous Howard projects, *Apollo 13* and *How the Grinch Stole Christmas*, and Howard knew that he had both the passion and the talent to bring *The Alamo* to life.

In April 2002, Howard, Hallowell, and Corenblith met with seven Alamo historians and authors in a marathon summit meeting in Austin, Texas—James Crisp, Jesús Francisco de la Teja, Stephen L. Hardin, Ph.D., Stephen Harrigan, Alan C. Huffines, Frank Thompson, Andres Tijerina, and Bruce Winders. The purpose of the meeting was to ensure that the film would stick as close as possible to history, deviating from the facts only for dramatic effect.

11

Howard eventually decided not to direct the film, choosing instead to serve only as producer, but the dedication to authenticity and accuracy on *The Alamo* never wavered.

When John Lee Hancock entered the picture, he felt it was important for him to make his own pass at the material after the work of Bohem and Stephen Gaghan, who had recently won an Academy Award® for his screenplay for *Traffic*. A successful screenwriter himself (*A Perfect World, Midnight in the Garden of Good and Evil*), Hancock had definite ideas about the themes and ideas he wanted to present in *The Alamo*, but was eager to keep the best elements of what had come before.

"Les wanted to de-mythologize the whole story and make these characters flesh-and-blood," Hancock says. "And, for me, it's all about characters." The earlier screenplay drafts offered "a unique perspective from the Mexican side in addition to some lesser known defenders at the Alamo [as well as] the political perspective of what was happening in Mexico at the time, which was necessary—great stuff for our story."

Hancock worked to humanize the characters of Bowie, Travis, and Crockett, the "holy trinity" of the Alamo who are too often idealized as flawless heroes. Each of the characters travels his own journey through the course of the film: Bowie comes home to Bexar to make peace with his past; Travis grows into a leader of men; and Crockett confronts his personal duality—the man and the legend, "David" vs. "Davy." According to Hancock, "Stephen Gaghan personalized Travis in a way that was historically accurate and quite telling in the arc of his character."

From the first draft of the first screenplay, *The Alamo* was always an inclusive look at the subject, in which the characters on both sides of the conflict were viewed with equal sympathy—and scrutiny.

Production designer Michael Corenblith says, "There's an old adage that period movies will always tell you more about the period in which they were made than the period they depict. And so in the same way that the John Wayne movie in 1960 was really formed by the Cold War, by America's place in the world, this new movie is inescapably part of its time, which is a far more multicultural and multidimensional world than it was forty years ago."

Even though the fate of the project seemed in

12

doubt when Howard left and Hancock arrived, construction of the massive sets of the Alamo and San Antonio de Bexar were already well underway on a vast ranch in Dripping Springs, Texas, about thirty miles west of Austin.

Hancock says, "The sets are just fantastic. Michael Corenblith is a genius. It is wonderful, after spending a lot of time in San Antonio at the real Alamo, and trying to envision that as a fortress, to finally see it like this and be able to walk around it. I'm a kid who gets to play in the biggest sandbox in the world."

Playing in that sandbox along with Hancock were producer Mark Johnson and executive producer Philip Steuer, cinematographer Dean Semler and actors Dennis Quaid (Sam Houston), Billy Bob Thornton (David Crockett), Jason Patric (James Bowie), Jordi Molla (Juan Seguin), Emilio Echevarria (Santa Anna), and Patrick Wilson (William Barret Travis).

Production began on January 27, 2003. Corenblith's massive sets were soon filled with hundreds of costumed and uniformed extras, horses, cattle, oxen, goats, chickens, and every other detail essential to bringing this world of 1836 to life. Filming would not be completed until Friday, June 13—101 days later. The last scene filmed showed Santa Anna's army marching slowly through the still-smoldering ruins of Gonzales.

Over the course of that 101 days, cast and crew endured weather of almost every description. The first day's temperature in central Texas was a biting 22 degrees. The last scenes were filmed on a day when the thermometer hit a scorching 102 degrees. In between, there was snow, sleet, freezing rain, heavy humidity, and dust storms. Hancock characterizes the production as, "From frostbite to sunstroke."

Oscar®-winner Dean Semler and his crew exposed 1,091,070 feet of film, more than was used on Disney's WWII film, *Pearl Harbor.* And the period muskets, flintlocks, and cannon burned over twice as much powder as was used during the production of Mel Gibson's Revolutionary War epic *The Patriot.*

Although often grueling for both cast and crew, the production of *The Alamo* was among the most positive

[Above right] Bexar's San Fernando Church under construction.
[Right] Mauricio Zatarain (center) gets direction from John Lee Hancock as the Mexican army sweeps into Bexar.

and enthusiastic experiences most of them could remember.

Billy Bob Thornton says, "I can't name one day on this set when there's been any tension that I know of," he says. "It's been a wonderful thing. John Lee Hancock is a hero in my book."

For the hundreds of extras, producer Mark Johnson said, *The Alamo* was "clearly not just a job, not just another movie. They are aware of the fact that they're making *The Alamo* and their commitment is above and beyond what you might normally expect of extras."

"You talk to any extra," says Stephen Hardin, "and they really feel privileged to be able to tell the story. This is really something for me, too. I'm supposed to be an objective, serious professor of history. But it's impossible to sit here and not get excited. And I think everybody who's part of this feels the same way."

To John Lee Hancock, "[*The Alamo*] may well be the most important movie I ever do." He says, "It's both an honor and quite daunting. I grew up with this story. My father took me there many times. And this is about never forgetting that little boy who stood at the Alamo."

[Left] John Lee Hancock directs Billy Bob Thornton on the Alamo set. [Below] A stalwart group of Texian and Tejano Alamo defenders.

THIRTEEN DAYS
THE SIEGE AND FALL OF THE ALAMO

In 1836, Texas was still a part of Mexico. The majority of people both inside the Alamo and surrounding it were Mexican citizens.

Over a decade earlier, the Mexican government sought to populate the huge region by opening its borders to settlers, offering families 4,428 acres if they agreed to stay in Texas for a full decade. In addition to the free land, the Constitution of 1824 offered the new Texians a decade without taxation.

For those settlers who flooded into Texas from all parts of the United States and Europe, the promise of the territory seemed limitless. Vast ranges of fertile land, mighty rivers, abundant game—Texas offered everything a newcomer needed to build a bright future.

But by 1830, Mexico started closing its borders. The country's new president and dictator, General Antonio López de Santa Anna, abolished the Constitution of 1824. No new settlers were allowed into Mexico; those already there and who had become Mexican citizens were no longer excused from paying taxes.

Almost three quarters of the new Texians had come from the United States. Even though they had become Mexican citizens, most of them still thought of themselves as Americans—and some of the most radical of them began advocating Texian independence from Mexico.

The first shots were fired at Gonzales. The Mexican army demanded the return of a small cannon that had been left in the town. The men from Gonzales shouted "Come and take it," fired the cannon at the Mexicans, and sent them running for their lives.

Santa Anna sent General Martin Perfecto de Cos to San Antonio de Bexar, the largest and most important city in Texas. Cos and his troops occupied an old Spanish mission just across the river from town. Once known as Mission San Antonio de Valero, most people now knew it as the Alamo. Cos and his 1400 men began fortifying the mission, believing that from their

position of strength, they could put down the revolt before it really started.

But they didn't count on the fury and determination of the Texians, who numbered only about three hundred. On December 5, 1835, they engaged the Mexicans in savage house-to-house fighting in Bexar. And when the Mexicans retreated to the Alamo, the Texians quickly forced them to surrender. By December 9, it was all over and Cos and his army were riding back toward Mexico, their tails between their legs. In surrendering, Cos's men

were allowed to keep their arms for protection on the condition that they would never return to Texas.

Santa Anna was furious. He began marching north with his army. And when he met Cos along the way, he ordered the embarrassed general to turn around and return with him to Bexar.

Meanwhile, with Cos gone, the Texians in Bexar set about finishing what he had started: the fortification of the Alamo. Commander J. C. Neill put amateur architect Green B. Jameson in charge of overseeing the remodeling. Despite the fact that a thousand of Cos's men couldn't defend the place against three hundred Texians, Jameson was confident that the Texians could hold the Alamo "ten to one" against the enemy.

But Jameson worried that the odds would be even worse than that. The Texians had started with three hundred men, but many of them left as soon as the siege of Bexar was over. Some assumed that the war was over. Others joined an ill-fated expedition to Matamoros, Mexico, which hoped to combine victory with plunder. Neill himself left to see to family business leaving William Barret Travis and James Bowie in uneasy co-command.

Travis was a former lawyer from South Carolina. Bowie was already notorious for his many exciting exploits and, more especially, for the monstrous knife which bore his name. But there was one in the fort even more famous than Bowie—David Crockett. He was a former Congressman from Tennessee but was better known for his exploits as an Indian fighter and bear hunter.

On February 23, 1836, Santa Anna's army arrived in Bexar and the Texians retreated to the Alamo. Santa Anna demanded unconditional surrender and flew a blood red flag meaning "no quarter" from the bell tower of San Fernando Church in Bexar's main plaza.

Travis answered the demand for surrender with a cannon shot. The Mexicans immediately began bombarding the fort and continued to do so virtually around the clock. No one inside the Alamo was killed in the bombardment but they were unable to rest. Soon they were exhausted, their nerves shattered.

Travis sent out some fifteen couriers with letters asking for reinforcements. The most famous of these was written on the second day of the siege.

18

To the People of Texas &
All Americans in the world—
Fellow citizens and compatriots–

I am besieged by a thousand or more of the Mexicans under Santa Anna—I have sustained a continual bombardment & cannonade for 24 hours & have not lost a man—the enemy has demanded a surrender at discretion, otherwise the garrison are to be put to the sword, if the fort is taken—I have answered the demand with a cannon shot, and our flag still waves proudly from the walls—I shall never surrender or retreat. Then, I call on you in the name of Liberty, of patriotism & everything dear to the American character to come to our aid with all dispatch—The enemy is receiving reinforcements daily and will no doubt increase to three or four thousand in four or five days. If this call is neglected, I am determined to sustain myself as long as possible & die like a soldier who never forgets what is due to his own honor and that of his country.

Victory or death.

William Barret Travis
Lt. Colonel Comdt.

P. S. The Lord is on our side—when the enemy appeared in sight we had not three bushels of corn—we have since found in deserted houses 80 or 90 bushels & got into the walls 20 or 30 head of Beeves.

Travis

Travis's appeals probably brought only a single response—thirty-two men from the town of Gonzales, where the revolution had begun (some historians believe a second group of reinforcements, possibly about sixty men, entered the fort on March 5). The Gonzales men were welcome, but there weren't nearly enough of them

James Butler Bonham, a fellow South Carolinian who had known Travis in boyhood, rode for help and returned to the Alamo with a message of hope. But Travis

[Above right] Cinematographer Dean Semler checks the light in Travis's headquarters as Patrick Wilson prepares for his scene.
[Right] A replica of one of William Barret Travis's eloquent letters from the Alamo.

19

feared that reinforcements wouldn't arrive in time. Legend has it that he gathered his men together, told them that they were doomed to die if they stayed in the Alamo, and drew a line in the dirt with his sword. He asked every man willing to stay with him and fight to the death to cross the line. Only a single man, the legend says, opted to go over the wall to seek safety.

On the evening of March 5, the bombardment stopped abruptly. The defenders of the Alamo, having been driven almost mad from the constant shelling over a period of two weeks, fell into a grateful sleep. Travis stationed sentries outside the wall and then tried to get some sleep himself.

But within hours, very early on the morning of March 6, the defenders of the Alamo were awakened by the blaring of bugles, the firing of guns and the shouts of thousands of Mexicans, crying "Viva Santa Anna!" and "Viva Republica!"

Travis jumped up from his bed, grabbed his shotgun and ran toward the north wall, followed by his slave Joe. Crockett and his men defended the wooden palisade beside the Alamo church. Jim Bowie, gravely ill

throughout most of the siege, was quartered in a room in the "low barracks" on the south side of the mission.

Inside the Alamo church, women and children, the families of the defenders, huddled in terror. Seven-year-old Enrique Esparza could see his father Gregorio at his post on the cannon ramp in the back of the church. Lt. Almeron Dickinson manned the cannon alongside Esparza. His wife and baby daughter, Susanna and Angelina Dickinson, were with the Esparzas and others.

Travis was among the first Texians killed in the battle, brought down by a single shot to the forehead. He died in a sitting position beside his cannon as the Mexican soldiers rushed past him into the Alamo compound.

The largest cannon in the Alamo was located in the southwest corner of the fort. As the Mexicans swept into the Alamo, the Texians turned the cannon around and fired it into the onrushing mass. Many Texians retreated to the long barracks where they had fortified the individual rooms. They were determined to fight it out man to man, if need be. When the Texians at the big cannon were overwhelmed, the Mexicans aimed it at the doors of the long barracks and the Alamo church,

Alamo families. Both the Hispanic Esparza family (left) and the Anglo Dickinson family (right) endured the siege. The two men were killed in the battle.

The earliest known depiction of the battle of the Alamo, first published in 1837. [Author's Collection]

destroying Texians with their own shot and shell.

Bowie was probably very close to death from illness when the Mexicans burst into his room and perforated him with bayonets.

Crockett's men at the palisade retreated toward the church to make their last stand. They were overpowered. On the cannon ramp, Esparza, Dickinson, and the rest were riddled with gunfire. Perhaps the last sounds they heard were the screams of their own families from the room at the foot of the ramp.

Gradually, the savage hand-to-hand fighting slowed to a stop. Mexican soldados, enraged by the brutal fight, wandered through the Alamo compound, finishing off wounded Texians, and mutilating those who were already dead. A few survivors, wounded and exhausted, were found. Although the gallant General Castrillón urged Santa Anna to take the men prisoners, Santa Anna demanded that they be put to death. Many believe that David Crockett was among these prisoners, but that controversy may never be settled.

The sun rose over the Alamo to reveal a horrifying scene. The blood-soaked ground was littered with hundreds of bodies. Santa Anna gazed about with satisfaction. When congratulated on his victory, he responded with a modest shrug. "It was but a small affair," he said.

The bodies of the slain Texians were stacked in three funeral pyres and burned. The battle of the Alamo was over.

1835:

OCTOBER 2— The "Come and Take It!" fight at Gonzales—the first shots of the Texas Revolution.

OCTOBER 3— Santa Anna gains control over the Mexican government and abolishes the Constitution of 1824.

OCTOBER 9— General Martin Perfecto de Cos occupies San Antonio de Bexar.

DECEMBER 5–9— The Texians attack Cos and his army, first fighting house-to-house in Bexar, then besieging them in the Alamo.

DECEMBER 10— Cos surrenders to the Texians and leaves Bexar, pledging to never again bear arms against Texas.

DECEMBER 21— Colonel James C. Neill is appointed to command the garrison at Bexar by Sam Houston.

DECEMBER 31— Santa Anna begins assembling his army and prepares to march to Bexar.

1836:

January 19— James Bowie arrives in Bexar, perhaps with orders from Houston to destroy the Alamo and the fortifications in town.

February 3— William Barret Travis arrives in Bexar with his cavalry unit, numbering about thirty men.

February 8— David Crockett arrives in Bexar with a company he has joined, informally known as the "Tennessee Mounted Volunteers."

February 11— Neill leaves Travis in command.

February 14— Travis and Bowie agree to command together. Bowie is ill.

February 23— Santa Anna's army enters Bexar. The Texians take refuge in the Alamo.

February 24— Bowie's illness worsens, causing him to turn over command solely to Travis.

Mexican cannons begin bombarding the Alamo.

Travis writes his famous "To the People of Texas" letter.

February 25— A few Texians venture outside the Alamo's walls to burn some jacales that have offered cover to Mexican soldiers.

February 26— Fannin and his men return to Goliad due to equipment problems.

Mexican cavalry attack the east side of the Alamo and are driven off by the Texians.

February 27— James Butler Bonham rides out with a message to Fannin.

THE ALAMO
DAY BY DAY

March 1—	Thirty-two men from Gonzales arrive at the Alamo.
March 2—	At Washington-on-the-Brazos, the delegates ratify the Texas Declaration of Independence.
March 3—	Bonham returns to the Alamo.
	More Mexican reinforcements arrive.
March 4—	Sam Houston is appointed commander in chief of the Texian forces.
March 5—	Santa Anna decides to storm the Alamo.
	The bombardment ceases.
	James Allen rides out with more messages.
March 6—	The Mexican army attacks the Alamo at around 5 A.M. The battle lasts for about an hour. All the Texians in the fort are killed.
March 10—	Santa Anna splits his army into four sections, leaving one in Bexar and sending the rest to various points in Texas to defeat Texians along the way.
March 13—	Susanna Dickinson, her daughter Angelina and Travis's slave, Joe, arrive in Gonzales where they deliver the news of the fall of the Alamo to Houston.
March 14—	Houston burns Gonzales, then leads his army east.
March 19—	Fannin and his men once again leave Goliad. They get about ten miles when they are attacked by the Mexicans under General Urrea.
March 20—	Fannin surrenders and the prisoners are led back to Goliad.
March 27—	Fannin's men are split into three groups, marched a short distance from the Mission La Bahia and executed. A few men escape.
April 20—	The armies of Houston and Santa Anna camp only a few miles from each other near San Jacinto. They clash briefly but Houston will not allow his men to fight. The Mexicans set up camp about 1,000 yards from Houston's army.
April 21—	General Cos arrives to reinforce Santa Anna, bringing the army's total to about 1,500.
	At about 4 P.M., the Texians attack, surprising the Mexicans. Shouting "Remember the Alamo!" and "Remember Goliad!" the vengeful Texians kill some 650 Mexicans in about eighteen minutes. Santa Anna flees the scene.
April 22—	Santa Anna, dressed as a private, is captured and brought before Houston. Though many Texians advocate hanging the dictator, Houston accepts his surrender and demands that all Mexican armies in Texas retreat to south of the Rio Grande. Santa Anna agrees, clearing the way for Texas to establish itself as a Republic, independent of Mexico.

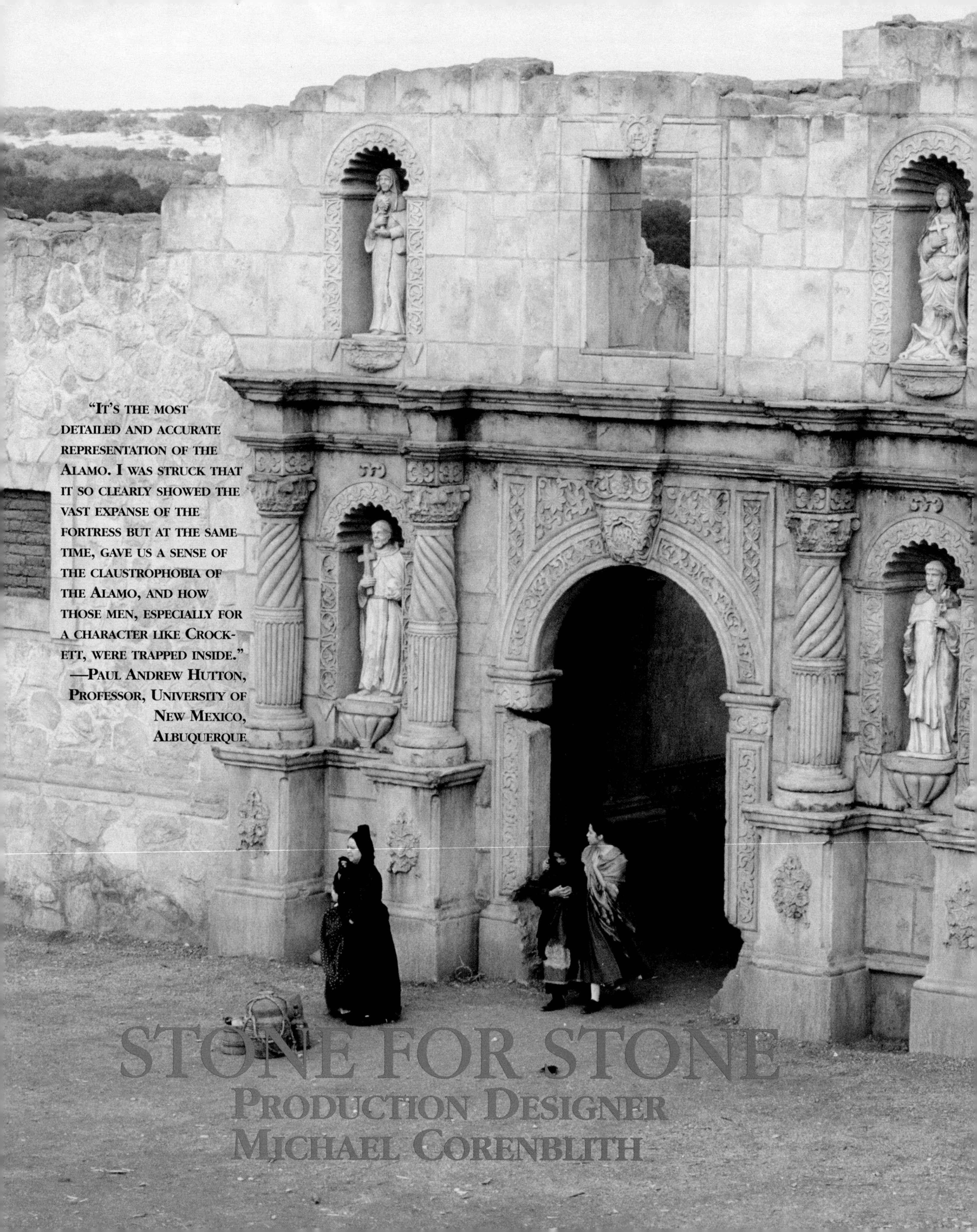

"It's the most detailed and accurate representation of the Alamo. I was struck that it so clearly showed the vast expanse of the fortress but at the same time, gave us a sense of the claustrophobia of the Alamo, and how those men, especially for a character like Crockett, were trapped inside."
—Paul Andrew Hutton, Professor, University of New Mexico, Albuquerque

Stone for Stone

Production Designer Michael Corenblith

Michael Corenblith was virtually the first artist hired to work on *The Alamo*. The production designer, who received Academy Award® nominations for *Apollo 13* and *How the Grinch Stole Christmas*, was first approached in 1998. However, it wasn't until October 2000 that he began working in earnest on the set designs for the film.

"At that point," Corenblith says, "the script that I was really working from were the history books. The sets really hadn't been conceived in response to a particular screenplay. The screenplay was always in flux. That gave me a great amount of freedom, to plan these sets based on history—not on a script or a director's vision."

What Corenblith was faced with building was not only the Alamo, a sprawling mission compound, already over 100 years old when the film begins, but also the entire town of San Antonio de Bexar. In addition, he would build the towns of Gonzales and San Felipe, a Cherokee Indian Village and the campsites of the warring Texian and Mexican armies at San Jacinto.

His crew would eventually number some 300 artists and craftsmen—only 25 of whom came from outside Texas. He and his small army spent almost eight months erecting over seventy buildings. After scouting locations all over the western United States and Canada, a sprawling ranch near Austin, Texas, was chosen to build the sets.

In 1836 San Antonio de Bexar sat across the river from the Alamo, about a half mile away. Looking out from town, the Alamo was off to the left. One of Corenblith's first artistic decisions was to bring both the town and the fort into line. And because the camera lens tends to exaggerate distances, the two sets were built a quarter of a mile apart.

He says, "It was my idea that the town of Bexar and the events in the Alamo are equally related. A lot of the sight lines between the town and the Alamo were conceived and created to be a single event. So if you bisect the center line of those doors in San Fernando Church, you can draw a line straight down to one of the apertures in the west wall of the Alamo."

Corenblith continues, "Sometimes my responsibilities to the filmmakers and to the movie audience will occasionally overshadow or trump my responsibilities to history. It is a creative process, after all, and everything that one puts on the screen is ultimately indicative of a choice that one has to make."

The most controversial bit of dramatic license in Corenblith's Alamo set is the position of the most famous building in Alamo—the church. It is this building that survives today in San Antonio, along with a fragment of the formerly two-story structure known as the long barracks.

Corenblith made the decision to move the church

An eight-year-old Michael Corenblith (right) poses in the icon niche of the real Alamo in San Antonio. (Left) All grown up, Corenblith poses in the set he meticulously re-created in Dripping Springs.

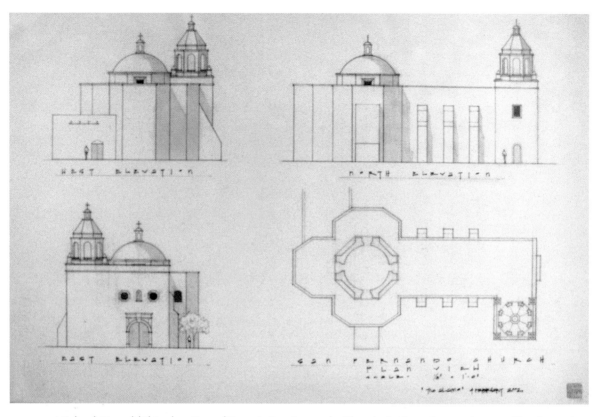

Michael Corenblith's elevation of Bexar's San Fernando Church, built to the precise specifications of the original building.

up about eighty feet, knowing that the façade is among the most famous in the world. Corenblith says, "What this has enabled us to do is to make the icon accessible throughout the plaza, so that the audience understands where they are at all times."

John Lee Hancock agrees. He says, "When I saw it, I thought, 'You know what? Not only can I live with it, I think it's the right idea.' The church is the emotional architectural center of the story. It'd be a damned shame not to see it for 95 percent of the movie."

Although Corenblith made some changes in the broad strokes, his attention to the details has been meticulous. He and his staff not only scoured every history of the Alamo for clues as to color and texture, they examined all kinds of buildings of the period. The result, he says, is that "we can say, without contradiction, that there are no details, there are no colors, there are no building forms that you see out here that we can't point to a painting or an etching or a rendering from the period, from the region, from the time, and point directly to that resource."

In addition to carefully studying all existing drawings and paintings of the Alamo and Bexar from the period, he consulted with the leading authorities on the subject,

California's Craig Covner, Texas's George Nelson and New York's Gary Zaboly. Each of these artists has done his own in-depth research and the paintings and drawings they produced proved invaluable to Corenblith.

A stickler for historical detail, Zaboly approves of what Corenblith accomplished. "The church itself is a marvelous facsimile of the 1836 original," he says. "Unlike John Wayne's version, this new construction not only gives us its true, severely irregular and rubbled roofline, but seems to have duplicated the façade of the actual building stone for stone. It is an incredible feat of workmanship. All four of its niches contain statues of the saints: a feature corroborated by the first post-battle sketches of the ruin in the late 1830s. The reconstructed San Fernando Church is no less splendid, and its painted walls indicate the depth of research engaged in by Corenblith and his designers."

For Michael Corenblith, building the Alamo has been more than just a job—it has been an obsession. He smiles and remembers, "When our historians finally arrived on the set, one of them came to me and said, 'Are you aware that you have created this properly and correctly, stone for stone?'

"And my answer was, 'Why wouldn't we?'"

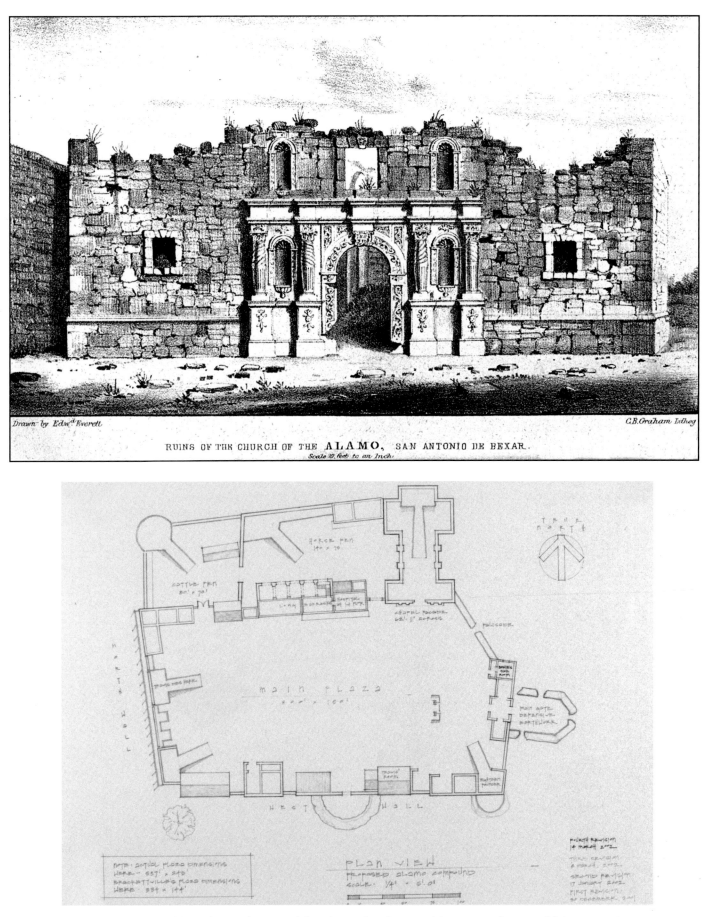

[Above] An early, highly authentic drawing of the Alamo church, one of the sources for Corenblith's research.
[Below] Blueprint of the Alamo set.

"IT'S JUST LIKE A PLAYGROUND. IT DOESN'T FEEL LIKE A SET. YOU DON'T FEEL LIKE YOU'RE ACTING. I THINK IT ALL WORKS FOR US. IT ALL HELPS US OUT IN KEEPING EVERYTHING VERY REAL. IT'S VERY EASY TO PLAY WHEN YOU'RE FACED WITH THE REALITY OF IT. I THINK THAT'S THE GLORY OF THIS MOVIE, THAT IT'S SO REAL. THE SET IS SO REAL AND SO APPARENT."

—PATRICK WILSON (WILLIAM BARRET TRAVIS)

"He was an alcoholic," says Dennis Quaid. "He was bipolar, manic-depressive."

Quaid is speaking of Sam Houston. And if his assessment of the man he plays in *The Alamo* seems unduly harsh, Quaid immediately tempers it with a more positive pronouncement: "He was also a great man."

SAM HOUSTON

Dennis Quaid has spent a lifetime admiring Sam Houston. "I myself am a Texan," he says. "I'm from Houston, in fact, so this story and this character resonates even more for me. I just feel so lucky to be here doing it. Growing up, we used to play The Alamo. We used to play the Battle of San Jacinto. And now I'm all grown up, and now we've got all these great toys to play with. It's a lot more fun."

Sam Houston has been called the father of Texas, the hero of San Jacinto, and "a broken-down sot and debauchee." Like many new Texians, he came to the territory stained by scandal, disappointment, and failure, determined to build a better future for himself. Unlike many of them, he actually succeeded. His defeat of Santa Anna at San Jacinto—the battle where the cry "Remember the Alamo!" was born—won Texas's independence and transformed the massive territory into its own Republic. Houston served two terms as the first popularly elected president of the Republic of Texas. And when Texas joined the United States in 1846, Houston became, with Thomas Jefferson Rusk, one of its first two senators.

Debate still rages among historians as to whether Houston was a brilliant tactician or a ne'er-do-well who only attacked at San Jacinto under pressure from his own troops. But no one denies that he was a colorful, adventurous, often infuriating figure with a knack for being where the action was.

"Sam was a hard person to like," says Quaid. "He had demons within himself that he was always dealing with. He had to make some tough decisions in his life."

On April 21, 1836, six weeks after the fall of the Alamo, Houston and his army attacked Santa Anna at San Jacinto. Six hundred and fifty Mexicans were killed in a bloody melee that lasted only eighteen minutes. Only six Texians were killed.

Quaid says, "I went to San Jacinto with Alan Huffines and Dr. Steve Hardin, the historians who are helping us out here. We walked the entire battle field. I went there as a kid but it was never illuminated for me like it was this time, to realize just how it all played out, and how brutal that it was. They fought with their bare hands, their rifles butts, knives…it got out of con-

trol in a way. This is not what you get in the history book."

The victory at San Jacinto made Houston a hero in the eyes of the Texians. He served as a senator from Texas until 1859, and was again elected governor of Texas. As the Civil War approached, Houston bitterly opposed secession, and resigned as governor rather than join the Confederate States of America. He died in the middle of that war, on July 26, 1863.

"He came here to Texas to start over again, like so many people did." Dennis Quaid says of Houston. "And he wound up carving out a nation. For me it's the chance of a lifetime to play this role."

DAVID CROCKETT

David Crockett is the most famous member of the Alamo garrison today. His legendary exploits have been celebrated in plays, novels, poems, movies, and songs.

He has been portrayed on the screen by actors as diverse as Fess Parker, John Wayne, and Mac Davis. His coonskin cap is an indelible symbol of the frontier era; it holds a special place in pop culture, too, as the Baby Boom generation bought and wore the headgear by the millions during the "Crockett Craze" of the 1950s.

But, unlike the other defenders of the Alamo, who became famous through their sacrifice, Crockett was already a legend by the time he arrived in San Antonio de Bexar. On the one hand, he was famous as a politician, having served two terms in the United States Congress. On the other, he was known as the ultimate frontiersman, a bear hunting, Indian fighting, tale-spinning, bigger-than-life figure who liked to say of himself that he was "half horse, half alligator with a little touch of snapping turtle."

Part of the Crockett legend came from a play by James Kirk Pauldings called "The Lion of the West." The lead character was a backwoods bumpkin named Nimrod Wildfire, but it was clear to everyone who saw it, that Nimrod was actually a lampoon of Congressman Crockett. Crockett himself was upset by the portrayal at first, but in 1833, he attended a performance in Washington by actor James Hackett, who played Nimrod. Hackett, who wore a preposterous fur hat and gaudy buckskins, stepped onto the stage that night and bowed deeply in Crockett's direction. Crockett bowed right back and the crowd went wild. It was at that moment that the real David and the legendary Davy were forever linked in the public's mind—and, to some extent, in Crockett's as well.

Thornton says, "Crockett didn't even wear a coonskin hat before that; that came from the play. And once he saw that, he took advantage of it. He wore it a few times after that when he was speaking to people, just kind of living up to the legend. But when he was watching the play, I'm sure he had mixed feelings. So, that was really the way I played it, as a guy who had mixed feelings about it."

David Crockett was born in Tennessee on August 17, 1786. Growing up, he didn't show much aptitude as either a farmer or a student, but he more than earned his keep as a hunter. He served briefly with the militia during the Creek Indian War, but was appalled by the horror of battle.

After the war, Crockett began his career in politics, serving as a magistrate, Justice of the Peace, and as colonel of the local militia. From there, it was on to the State Legislature and then, in 1827, to a seat in Congress.

Crockett served two terms but his stand in favor of Indians' rights caused him to be defeated in 1835 by Adam Huntsman, a man with a wooden leg. In a memorable farewell address, he said, "Since you have chosen to elect a man with a timber toe to succeed me, you may all go to hell and I will go to Texas!"

Crockett saw Texas as a land of promise. He believed that he could reinvent himself politically in the new land. And, to be on the safe side, he made sure that he took "legendary Davy" along with him. His daughter recalled that the last time she saw her father, he was standing on the deck of a steamship, "dressed in his hunting shirt and wearing a coon skin cap."

Legend has it that Crockett entered Texas at the head of his own company, the "Tennessee Mounted Volunteers." Actually, Captain William Harrison was the leader of the company—Crockett was just riding along. But that didn't stop people from thinking of the other men as "Crockett's boys." It's entirely possible that Capt. Harrison began to think so, himself. After all, the real and the legendary have always had a way of mixing themselves up in Crockett's life.

For the man who portrays David Crockett in *The Alamo*, there was a similar mixture of the real and the unreal. "It was fun for me 'cause I normally don't do a role like this," says Billy Bob Thornton. "Normally I play maybe parts of myself, but certainly not exactly myself. And in this one I kind of do that. Maybe the first time I've ever done that."

"BILLY BOB IS SO CROCKETT, IT'S SCARY. HE HAS THE SAME MAGNETISM CROCKETT HAD. ALL THESE OTHER GUYS ARE ACTING; HE'S CHANNELING."
STEPHEN L. HARDIN, PH.D.
HISTORICAL ADVISOR

WILLIAM BARRET TRAVIS

To actor Patrick Wilson, one of the keys to the personality of young William Barret Travis was that he only reluctantly came to be the commander of the Alamo. "Travis tried to get out of this job like three times," Wilson says. "He wrote to the governor, 'Please, I do not want to go to an old mission and sit there. Let me be out in the cavalry, let me do something.' He really kind of whined about it."

But, Wilson says, when Travis arrived at the Alamo, he began seeing things in a different light—and began the slow, painful process of coming into his own. "I think he got here and realized that he had the wrong idea about command. He thought being a leader meant he had to be very fancy and wear nice clothes and read all sorts of books on [Scottish hero] William Wallace. Once he's at the Alamo, you see him growing up, finding out who he is, ultimately at the expense of his death."

Travis did not enter the gates of the Alamo as a famous man, as James Bowie or David Crockett did. But through the bravery of his defense of the old mission and the eloquence and power of the letters he wrote during the siege, Travis became an equal member of that revered trinity. Director John Lee Hancock decided to cast the film in a similar way, with well-known actors Jason Patric and Billy Bob Thornton as Bowie and Crockett and cinema newcomer Patrick Wilson as Travis.

"I can't imagine anybody else playing the part," says John Lee Hancock. "Patrick is William Barret Travis. Travis at the start is a firebrand, a man who's idealistic. And over the course of two weeks, he comes from absolute obscurity, in terms of history—but for those two weeks, he certainly wouldn't be on a statue in San Antonio."

Of the three, Travis was perhaps the least likely one to attain the mantle of hero in his lifetime. Travis was born near Saluda, South Carolina, in 1809. His family moved to Alabama nine years later. A precocious student, Travis began teaching school in Claiborne, marrying one of his students, Rosanna Cato, when he was nineteen years old. Travis stopped teaching soon thereafter and began working in a law firm; he also published a newspaper, the *Claiborne Herald*.

The Travises' first child, Charles Edward, was born in 1829 and a daughter, Susan Isabella, followed a year later. But before she was born, Travis had already abandoned his family and headed for Texas. A persistent rumor is that Travis believed that Rosanna had been unfaithful to him and that he was not the father of the second child. Some historians have also suggested that he killed the man he believed to be responsible, then fled to Texas to avoid arrest.

In Texas, Travis started his own law office but as the flames of revolution began to grow hotter, he aligned himself with the "War Party," colonists who were in favor of fighting for independence from Mexico.

In Texas, he became engaged to Rebecca Cummings and pledged to marry her as soon as Rosanna granted him a divorce. Somehow, he convinced Rosanna to send their son Charles to Texas to live with him. When Charles arrived, Travis was too busy with the revolution and boarded the child with friends. Father and son never saw each other again.

Travis accepted a commission as a lieutenant of cavalry. When he was ordered to the Alamo, he protested bitterly. Still, he seems to have been a natural leader. And the letters he wrote during the siege remain the most authentic record of life inside the Alamo during those fateful thirteen days.

"He was very poetic," says Patrick Wilson. "He was a lawyer as well, so he was very profound, very, very smart. In the script, he wasn't written as a hero, he was written as a person with real problems. That was something that I felt like I could relate to. I don't know what it's like to feel like a hero. I approach it very realistically—this guy, assuming leadership, having problems with Bowie. Because Bowie's the crowd favorite and I'm the guy that a lot of people don't like. How do I make these guys like me and do I need them to like me? All those things are not hard to relate to."

Like David Crockett, James Bowie was already famous when he first stepped into the Alamo. Or, as Jason Patric's Bowie says to Crockett in *The Alamo*, "Not famous, notorious. There's a difference." Either way, the men of the Alamo and the people of Bexar knew him. Many feared him. Bowie was identified with the knife that bore his name but which he almost certainly had nothing to do with creating.

Bowie's exploits were legendary. Some of them were incredible, some despicable—and some of the more astonishing of them were actually true. Jason Patric says, "Bowie was a man of his time—an adventurer, a treasure hunter, a capitalist, a slave trader. I don't think he had a moral problem with it as a lot of people would." Indeed, Bowie lived much of his life on a moral tightrope. He was, after all, once partners with the pirate Jean Lafitte. "Just an all-around scoundrel I guess," says Patric.

Bowie was both intelligent and shrewd, but quick to anger. His fury, once unleashed, could be deadly. Perhaps his most famous encounter, before the Alamo, was the "Sandbar Fight" in Louisiana in 1827, a duel that turned into a brawl. Bowie was shot through the lung and in the thigh and stabbed several times. Nevertheless, he managed to kill a man with the large butcher knife that he carried. The story—and the knife—became so well known that men all over the territory began having their own "Bowie knives" manufactured for them.

He moved to Texas the following year, seeking adventure there, too. Bowie became a Mexican citizen and married Maria Ursula Veramendi, the daughter of the governor of the territory, but tragedy soon struck. "Bowie was off on one of his expeditions when cholera killed his whole family, including his wife," Jason Patric says.

40

Shattered by Ursula's death, Bowie flung himself wholeheartedly into the struggle for Texian independence. He led the Texians to victory at the battle of Concepción near Bexar in 1835. And he later returned there under orders from Houston to determine the fate of the fortifications in San Antonio and the Alamo itself. Once there, he chose to defend the Alamo, not destroy it, a decision that historians have struggled to understand ever since.

"My choice is that there was a nostalgic sort of feeling to his return to Bexar," says Jason Patric. "As his own last days were waning away, this is the only place he ever really felt comfortable. In a way, to blow up the Alamo and take these guns away and leave the rest of these townspeople with nothing was something that he couldn't really stomach."

As the siege of the Alamo began, Bowie shared command with Travis. But illness, perhaps typhoid, soon took Bowie out of the fight.

Although Jason Patric's performance brings out Bowie's humanity in full dimension, that doesn't mean he views the character as a particularly sympathetic one. And *The Alamo's* director doesn't either. Hancock says, "I never want anybody in the audience to think we're asking you to love Jim Bowie. We want you to think he's fascinating. We didn't want to back away from any of the warts and all. We wanted to make sure that everybody understood that he'd been a slave trader, and a land speculator, and all these things. And we still wanted people to think at the end of the movie, 'There's a little more to this guy than we thought. I hate him—but there's just something real interesting about him.'"

JAMES BUTLER BONHAM

Texas regards all of the defenders of the Alamo as heroes. But James Butler Bonham may have been the most heroic of all. Some fifteen couriers were sent out by Travis with letters appealing for reinforcements. Fourteen of them never returned. But as Bonham prepared to ride out of the Alamo, he is said to have declared to Travis, "I will report the results of my mission or die in the attempt!" And he did. According to legend, he came back with a bleak message—there would be no help. The men of the Alamo were doomed.

New evidence suggests that Bonham actually returned to the Alamo with a more hopeful message that several groups of reinforcements were on the way. But even if he was not the bearer of bad tidings, Bonham's bravery is undimmed. He knew that the situation at the Alamo was grim and that to return there was dangerous in the extreme. But he placed a higher value on his own honor than he did on his life.

Bonham, like Travis, was born near Saluda, South Carolina. Also like Travis, Bonham became a lawyer and eventually moved to Alabama, where he began taking an interest in the subject of Texas independence. He may have entered the Alamo with Bowie's volunteers, but soon rode out again as a courier, on February 16, 1836. He returned on March 3, just three days before the final assault.

His post during the battle is unknown. Some have suggested that he worked with the cannon crew on the ramp at the rear of the Alamo church. Others believe he manned a cannon position on the west wall.

It is at the latter position where *The Alamo* places Bonham. Actor Marc Blucas has vivid memories of defending Bonham's post. "It was a four-by-four window, with a Navy cannon sticking out of it," he recalls. "There were three of us working the cannon and three other guys were handing rifles around. And we have a moment where we look out, and there's about 2,000 people coming for the hole. I would like to say, hey, I'm a brilliant actor," Blucas laughs, "but there's no challenge at all when I see 2,000 people coming at me, shooting me—it was very easy to start grabbing guns and try to start shooting back.

"It was a horrific sight, even to be a part of it as an actor," he says. "And to try to imagine what really went down that night in 1836…I was scared out of my mind."

SANTA ANNA

When the men of the Alamo saw Santa Anna's red flag flying from the bell tower of San Fernando church, they knew at once what it meant—no quarter. Worse, they knew that it was no idle threat. General Antonio López de Santa Anna Pérez de Lebron was already known for his heartless approach to battle.

Many of them would have known of his suppression of a revolt in Zacatecas only months earlier. After defeating the rebels, he had many of the survivors executed by firing squad. And some of them—especially the handful of survivors brought before him after the battle of the Alamo—would learn that when he said "no prisoners," he meant it.

When it came to casting this mercurial and tempestuous dictator, John Lee Hancock had only one favorite—Emilio Echevarría, who delivered extraordinary performances in such international hits as *Y Tu Mamá También* (2001) and *Amores Perros* (2000). He had also, coincidentally, already portrayed Santa Anna in a theatrical production in 1985.

"When you cut to Santa Anna, he's got to hold the screen," Hancock says. "It would be really easy to cast somebody who's just a demon—but no antagonist is interesting until he does something that is almost kind—that takes you aback. I thought, 'That's what we need—someone you can't take your eyes off, an actor that jumps off the screen.' That's Emilio."

The general who called himself the "Napoleon of the West" believed in total victory, without terms, without mercy. "In Mexico, in the official histories," Echevarría says, "Santa Anna is stigmatized. He is condemned, seen as a villain. He's seen as the character responsible for the loss of the territory that subsequently became part of The United States." Neither Echevarría nor Hancock dispute the dictator's evil side, but both were determined to create a more complex portrayal of the often-reviled general than had been seen in previous films.

Echevarría resisted portraying Santa Anna as a one-dimensional villain in part because Mexico often viewed him with admiration. "This history that condemns him *a priori*," Echevarría says, "seems like a partial vision. What were the reasons for Santa Anna being elected president of Mexico so many times? One has to see the light and dark in this character. It seems to me that part of him was very popular—he could be a man of the people. He was from Veracruz, he officiated at the cock fights—he could be very, very likeable for a certain strata of the population."

In later years, Santa Anna served as president of Mexico three more times, lost a leg during the "Pastry War" with France, commanded forces during the Mexican War, was defeated at Cerro Gordo by General Winfield Scott, and helped to invent chewing gum.

Santa Anna died there in poverty in Mexico City on June 21, 1876.

45

GENERAL
MANUEL
CASTRILLON

Few scholars who study the Texas Revolution don't have a warm spot in their hearts for General Manuel Castrillón. He was extraordinarily brave, a man of honor and compassion. In most of the eyewitness accounts that describe the capture and execution of Texian survivors after the battle of the Alamo, it is Castrillón who goes before Santa Anna to plead for mercy. Earlier, he urged Santa Anna to hold off on attacking the Alamo, in order to save Mexican lives. And at San Jacinto, when Santa Anna and other top-ranking officers fled the field before Houston's vengeful army, Castrillón met his death with courage and dignity.

Dramatically, says John Lee Hancock, Castrillón (played by Argentine actor Castulo Guerra) serves an important function in *The Alamo*. "I just love the idea of a guy who has rules," Hancock says. "I'm really drawn to the idea of morals in war. Guys who say, 'No, this is the way things are done. You're a gentleman or you're not.' Castrillón is great for being a Greek chorus and/or serving to throw questions to Santa Anna. But I also think he ends up being the moral bellwether for the Mexican side."

Castrillón was born in Cuba. As a youth, he joined the Spanish army and came to Mexico with that invading force. Once there, he switched sides and began serving with Santa Anna. His intelligence and compassion often put him at odds with Santa Anna, but the general admired Castrillón and relied upon his judgment—when it suited him. Castrillón, in turn, deeply admired Santa Anna's military genius, even as he

deplored the dictator's barbarous and bloodthirsty nature.

After the Alamo, Castrillón remained with Santa Anna. He advised the general against making camp at San Jacinto, believing that the marshes and lake made it a trap from which it would be impossible to escape under attack. Santa Anna, of course, didn't believe that Houston would attack and so ignored Castrillón's warning.

Santa Anna was wrong, costing him the battle—and Texas—and costing Castrillón his life. But even in his last moments, Castrillón was the very model of courage and honor. He watched with dismay as Santa Anna fled the field. But although urged to run away himself, Castrillón is said to have folded his arms and glared at the advancing Texians who were about to kill him. "I've been in forty battles and never showed my back," he said. "I'm too old to do it now."

"Castulo and I had great discussions about his relationship with Santa Anna," Hancock says. "I said, 'I don't want you to play it as though you're the thorn in Santa Anna's side. By the end, when you're at San Jacinto and you see him leave and there's that look between you, I don't want it to be, 'I knew it! You coward!' I want it to be disappointment. I want it to be, 'I've given so much of my life in service of this man and he wasn't necessarily worth it.' I think that's heartbreaking—and it ends up making us fascinated by Castrillón. He's the most straight-up guy in the movie."

JUAN SEGUIN

Many of the actors in *The Alamo* chose to do extensive research into their characters. But Jordi Molla, a native of Spain who plays the central Tejano figure Juan Seguin, said that he came to the film knowing "Nothing, absolutely nothing," about the historical figure he portrays. For past roles, he says, he has undertaken to learn all he could about his character and the era depicted. But, Molla says, "Sometimes I want to know, sometimes I don't want to know. And this time I wanted to create my own Juan Seguin just talking to the director and looking at the other actors you know."

To Molla, Seguin is man caught in a conflict of conscience and loyalty. "He's with the American side, confused and guilty because he's killing his brothers. He's not agreeing with dictator Santa Anna. But at the same time he has always this question in his head—am I doing the right thing? He's fighting for something he's not really convinced about."

"We had long discussions where I would fill him in on what I knew about Seguin from my reading," John Lee Hancock says. "Jordi was having a hard time figuring Seguin's loyalties and affinities and then one day it clicked in. Jordi's a very well-known actor in Spain, and they're usually smaller movies. I think he and Javier Bardem are the guys that are also able to do both those films and big Hollywood movies. And he's very torn about that. He had just done *Bad Boys 2*, a big American movie and he was just torn. He said, 'They think I'm a traitor. Sometimes I wonder if they're not right.' He said, 'Now I understand. It's loyalty to country versus your own ideals. I try so hard to be loyal to

both. It's a hard place to be.' And I said, 'Yeah, I think that's Juan Seguin.'"

The real Juan Seguin was a man who knew all about the conflict between blood and conviction. Born in San Antonio in 1806, he followed in the footsteps of his politician father, first working in the post office, then serving as an alderman. Seguin was elected alcalde, or mayor, of Bexar in 1833.

Seguin bitterly opposed the Centralist regime of Santa Anna and led a militia company in 1835. He was commissioned as captain soon thereafter and formed his own company, numbering thirty-seven men, all Tejanos like himself. He and his men participated in the battle of Bexar when the Texians expelled General Cos's army from the Alamo. He served as translator during the surrender talks.

He and his men entered the Alamo with Travis and Bowie in February, but Seguin soon left as a courier. He remained with Houston after the fall of the Alamo and participated in the battle of San Jacinto.

A year after the battle of the Alamo, Seguin returned to Bexar to gather up the remaining ashes of the defenders. He delivered an impassioned eulogy, extolling the heroism of the men who died there.

Jordi Molla says, "The Alamo begins and ends with Juan Seguin, with his conflict. He looks at everything; he pays attention. But he does not agree a lot of the time. He feels frustration, he feels guilty, and he's always asking this question, over and over: 'Am I doing the right thing?'"

49

JOE AND
SAM

As one of the screenwriters and the director, John Lee Hancock was determined to make *The Alamo* as accurate and authentic as possible. But he realized that sometimes fiction is necessary in order to pave the clearest road to the truth. One example of this is the presence in *The Alamo* of Sam, the slave of James Bowie.

Although history shows that Alamo commander William Barret Travis brought a slave with him into the Alamo, a young man in his early twenties named Joe, there is no evidence that Bowie did. Interestingly, in the movies—from *Martyrs of the Alamo* (1915) to *Man from the Alamo* (1953) to John Wayne's *The Alamo* (1960), it is usually Bowie who is the slave owner. It is true that Bowie owned a slave named Sam, and that this manservant came to Texas with him, but there is scant evidence that he was present during the siege and fall of the Alamo. But Hancock believed that the presence of both slaves was required. Without Sam, Joe has no one he can speak freely with and no way to communicate to the audience the agonizing dilemmas faced by the two men. Therefore, in *The Alamo*, both men own slaves. It was, according to Hancock, the only way the audience could get that particular point of view.

"Joe [played by Edwin Hodge] is such a great character," Hancock says. "I like the idea of him kind of glomming onto the idealism of the man who 'holds his contract,' to Travis. And then he realized, 'This isn't my fight.' I wanted him to have someone he could talk to, someone older, wiser, who perhaps was once as idealistic as he was, or wanted to believe in his master so much, like Joe does."

Hancock continues, "I thought it was a strong idea to show these two slaves and their relationships with

50

their owners and with each other. Also, I thought it was disingenuous not to represent slavery as an aspect of the era."

Hancock says that he envisioned Sam as an angry, bitter man, anxious to be rid of his dour master—a logical enough interpretation under the circumstances. But Afemo Omilami, who played Sam, had a more complex idea. Hancock recalls, "Afemo said, 'Human beings are more complicated than that. Look at Stockholm Syndrome, look at Patty Hearst. You can't help it— you're going to want that person to appreciate you. And the more you're beaten down, you're like the dog that whimpers. I desperately want Jim Bowie, when I leave, to say thank you.'"

Hancock played the scene in which Sam leaves the Alamo as a subtle parody of a similar scene in John Wayne's *The Alamo*. In that film, on the eve of the battle, Bowie (Richard Widmark) gives his slave Jethro (Jester Hairston) his freedom. Hancock says, "There's a scene where some of the Tejanos have been offered amnesty by Santa Anna and they're leaving the fort. Bowie tells Sam to go with them. Sam is incredulous— 'You givin' me my papers?' Bowie says, 'No. I get off this bed, I'm gonna hunt you down!' We didn't want to play that at all—'Oh, you're a free man now'—we wanted to tease a little bit. But that's just it. When Sam looks back at Bowie at the door, he's giving this guy one more chance to say goodbye or thank you or something. And Afemo said to me, 'That's the heartbreak of it. I'm both guys. I'm the guy who's mad and bitter that I've spent my time with this guy. And I'm also the guy that desperately needs to please him.' And I thought, boy, that's what a smart actor'll do for you."

51

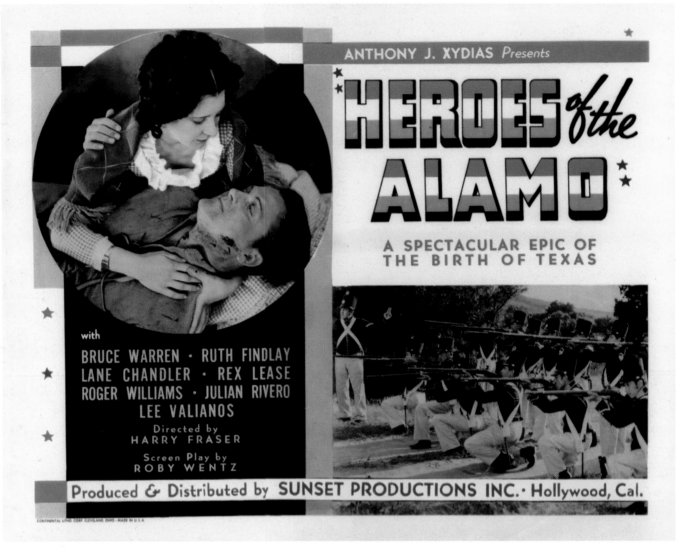

[Above] A lobby card from the 1937 B-movie *Heroes of the Alamo*. [Opposite, from top to bottom] Stills from the films *The Alamo: Shrine of Texas Liberty; Martyrs of the Alamo;* and *The Siege and Fall of the Alamo.*

The Alamo is by far the most accurate and authentic film ever made on the subject, but it is far from the first. There have been Alamo movies almost as long as there have been movies of any kind—dating all the way back to 1911.

Of the following films and television productions, only those marked with an asterisk (*) deal specifically with the siege and fall of the Alamo, either as the main focus of the story or as an important element (for instance, films about Sam Houston, such as *Man of Conquest*).

The others have significant scenes based at the Alamo, from Errol Flynn's moonlight shootout in the ruins of the old church in San Antonio to Pee-wee Herman's search for his bicycle in the Alamo's mythical basement in *Pee-wee's Big Adventure* to Sandra Bullock's beguiling musical glass solo in *Miss Congeniality.*

The Alamo shows up as a backdrop in many more films and television shows based in San Antonio, but those instances, which range from a concert sequence in *Selena* (1997) to the "Blame Canada" number from *South Park: Bigger, Longer and Uncut* (1999) are far too numerous to list here.

THE ALAMO ON FILM

- *The Immortal Alamo** (1911) Melies Star Film Company [now lost]
- *The Siege and Fall of the Alamo** (1913) Siege and Fall of the Alamo Company [now lost]
- *Martyrs of the Alamo: or The Birth of Texas** (1915) Triangle
- *Little Bluebonnet* (1922) San Antonio City Club [now lost]
- *With Davy Crockett at the Fall of the Alamo** (1926) Sunset
- *Tracy the Outlaw* (1928) Foto Art Productions
- *Remember the Alamo* (1935) Warner Bros.
- *Heroes of the Alamo** (1937) Sunset
- *The Alamo: Shrine of Texas Liberty** (1938) National Films/H.W. Kier
- *Land of Liberty** (1939) Motion Picture Producers and Distributors of America
- *Man of Conquest** (1939) Republic
- *San Antonio* (1945) Warner Bros.
- *The Man from the Alamo** (1953) Universal
- *Davy Crockett, King of the Wild Frontier** (1955) Disney
- *The Last Command** (1955) Republic
- *The Alamo** (1960) United Artists
- *Viva Max!* (1969) Commonwealth
- *Uncle Sam Magoo** (1970) UPA Productions

The battle ends in the very first Alamo movie, *The Immortal Alamo* (1911).

- ★ *Spirit of Independence** (1976) United States Government
- ★ *Seguin** (1982) PBS Television
- ★ *Frontier** [episode: "The Texicans"] (1956) NBC Television [now lost]
- ★ *You Are There** [episode: "The Defense of the Alamo"] (1953) CBS Television [now lost]
- ★ *Pontiac Star Parade: The Spirit of The Alamo** (1960) ABC Television
- ★ *Wagon Train* [episode: "The Jose Morales Story"] (1960) NBC Television
- ★ *The Time Tunnel** [episode: "The Alamo"] (1966) ABC Television
- ★ *You Are There** [episode: "The Siege of the Alamo"] (1971) CBS Television

- ★ *Wrong Is Right* (1982) Columbia
- ★ *Cloak and Dagger* (1984) Universal
- ★ *Pee-wee's Big Adventure* (1985) Warner Bros.
- ★ *Houston, the Legend of Texas** (video title: Gone to Texas) (1986) CBS Television
- ★ *Amazing Stories** [episode: "The Alamo Jobe"] (1986) NBC Television
- ★ *The Alamo: Thirteen Days to Glory** (1987) NBC Television
- ★ *The Alamo...the Price of Freedom** (1988) IMAX® Imax Corporation
- ★ *James A. Michener's Texas** (1995) ABC Television
- ★ *Two For Texas** (1998) Turner Network Television
- ★ *Miss Congeniality* (2000) Warner Bros.
- ★ *The Alamo** (2003) Disney

LIVING HISTORY

There are eighty-two principal characters in *The Alamo* with famous names like Crockett, Bowie, Houston, Travis, and Santa Anna.

But there are hundreds of characters in the movie whose names won't be listed in the credits and are never uttered in the film.

Indeed, these names are known to almost no one—except the person playing the role. Thanks to a color-coded book supplied by extra Cid Galindo, many of the extras portraying the Alamo defenders chose identities for themselves, just to make the experience more real. They made their choices based on age, background—or simply a gut feeling.

Galindo had already been cast as a Tejano defender, when he "happened to run into John Lee, the director, one night in Austin. He said, 'Hey, we ought to help you find a name.' John Lee encouraged me to do some more research and pointed me in some directions."

Galindo went online and found the website of the Daughters of the Republic of Texas, the curators of the Alamo in San Antonio. The website, Galindo says, "listed every man who fell at the Alamo as well as a short biography of what we knew about these guys. It was convenient, very well organized, and easy to work through."

Galindo printed out some 200 pages from the website, then organized them in alphabetical order and indexed them. "And then," he says, "I color-coded each name based on the groups that we were organized in here on the set. I was a Tejano, some guys were there with Crockett, there were the Travis guys, the guys from Gonzales and so on." As the extras looked through the book, they would focus on the color that designated their group. Galindo says, "All the Crockett guys were highlighted in green. If an extra was playing one of Crockett's men, he could go through the names and places of origin and narrow it down to two or three guys. Then he would read the bios and say, 'Okay, here's the guy I can relate to. Here's the guy that I want to play in this movie.'"

Texan Wayne Evans had a personal connection to the Texas Revolution. "My great, great grandfather's name was John W. McHorse," he says. "He fought in the Nacogdoches Company in the Battle of San Jacinto, signed up for the army the day the Alamo fell." But since McHorse didn't fight in the Alamo, Evans selected a defender who at least carried his family name—Robert Evans. "He was in charge of the ordnance," Evans says, "and at the end of the battle he was attempting to run to the powder room and blow it up."

Frank Masters, another Texan, chose as his character Joseph M. Hawkins, one of the volunteers under James Bowie. "I researched all the characters that we knew for sure were with Bowie's group. Hawkins was born in Ireland in 1799. He came to Texas by way of Louisiana. He was a big supporter of Texas independ-

ence, an express rider for General Sam Houston. And he was one of the men who rode into the Alamo with Bowie. He was 37 years old when he died."

Cid Galindo says, "I would say 90 percent of the extras have actually signed up for a name. If you were to ask any of them who they played in *The Alamo*, they would give you a name and they would know something about that person. And so it became very real for a lot of these guys."

The extras may have decided for themselves who they were going to be, but it was up to reenactor coordinator J. R. Flournoy to determine how they were going to conduct themselves. He and about 150 living history trainers drilled the two thousand extras in everything from marching to weapons handling to general period behavior. According to Flournoy; utilizing the most recent research into the 1836 period helps to ensure that *The Alamo* is as authentic as possible.

"We found an original copy of the 1830 Mexican military manual," he says. "It was what the Mexican troops used in 1836. We duplicated it and made it available to all of our trainers so that they could learn the proper drill of the period for the Mexican army, which was different from any other army. The best thing we had available a little over a year ago was the 1808 Spanish manual."

In addition, Flournoy and his San Antonio company

Historical Productions created a training manual of their own. He says, "It started out as a folder full of articles and pictures clipped from magazines, as well as other things people have written, and it's grown into the only manual of its kind in the United States. Ten years ago this show couldn't have been done as accurately as we're doing it today because we didn't have this knowledge."

All the extras and most of the principal actors underwent a three-day "boot camp" to learn how to load and fire the cannon and flintlock rifles in a period-correct way, and also to respond properly to military orders. The process, some of which was conducted in a driving rainstorm, was grueling. After the first day of marching through ankle-deep mud, many would-be extras had soon had enough and deserted.

But those who stayed did so for reasons that had little to do with money, or the glamour associated with appearing in a big Hollywood movie. "Most of them have a great interest in the Alamo," Flournoy says. "That's an advantage in itself. Because the ones that showed up and made the grade and were tough enough to make it through class wanted to be the Alamo defenders awful bad. So we've got people here from the east coast, the west coast, from all over the United States that have come here and really want to be a part of this show."

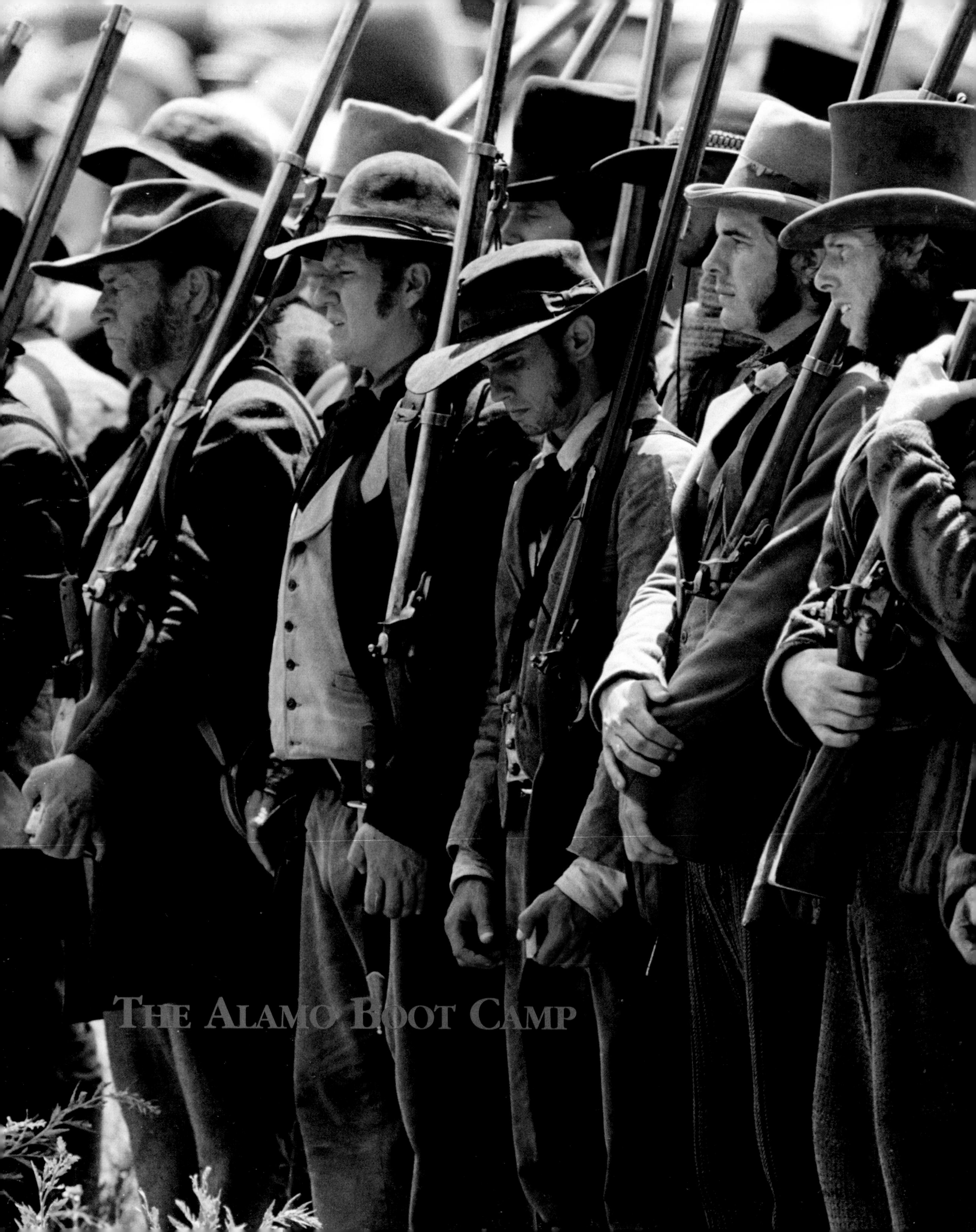

THE ALAMO BOOT CAMP

"The first day of training was cold and raining heavily. We were split into companies of thirty to forty guys, and marched for the first few hours. Some of the soldados and reenactors who were currently working in the Alamo portion of the movie trained us to march from Scott's Militia Abstract.

"We broke for lunch, which was chili...hot, spicy, and welcomed by all. After lunch we were introduced to the muskets for the first time. The rest of Day One was spent learning to give and take punches, get shot and fall—and more marching. At first we looked like the Keystone Cops. By day's end we began to resemble an army unit.

"Day Two was hot, sunny, and humid. More marching and stunt work. We broke for lunch with the promise of musket training—the favorite activity at 'The Alamo Fantasy Camp'—that afternoon.

"After a long morning of marching in the heat we were looking forward to sitting in an air-conditioned double-wide, sipping cool drinks and sampling the fine craft services grub we had heard would make up for the $15 we earned each day. What we got was leftover chili from Day One. More marching that afternoon—but we finally got to load and fire our muskets before they released us for the day.

"Day Three was hotter than Day Two. Marching, marching, and more marching. As we broke for lunch, there was a lot of funny banter about the fact that since we had eaten the rest of Day One's chili on Day Two... we were going to be rewarded. We were wrong. They made a whole new, fresh batch of chili. We spent the afternoon loading and firing our muskets on a dead run, simulating the undisciplined charge at San Jacinto.

"At the end of the day, each company mustered and marched up to the lunch trailer where J. R. Flournoy told some unlucky few that they would not be needed on the movie. He gave the rest of us a speech about what to expect—like no more chili on the set—and loaded us back into the buses.

"As we drove back on the bus to the parking lot, I couldn't help but reflect on that first bus ride on Day One. You could have heard a pin drop; everybody was quietly sizing each other up. But that ride back on Day Three was a bus filled with loud laughter, back-slapping, and a strong sense of camaraderie. We had all shared a special experience. The Alamo Fantasy Camp had ended. We were recruited into John Lee Hancock's Texian Army, and sent home to await our orders of deployment."

—Nick Newton, Texian Extra

[Right] Nick Newton, *left.*

59

From the beginning, the Alamo movies have had a tendency to prefer fiction over fact, "Hollywood" over history.

But this Alamo was different. Early in the project, producer Ron Howard and executive producer Todd Hallowell and production designer Michael Corenblith met with seven Alamo authorities in Austin to find out what it would take to make this the most authentic Alamo film ever made. Two of those historians, Alan C. Huffines and Stephen L. Hardin, Ph.D., would eventually be brought onto the project as, respectively, the military and historical advisors of *The Alamo*.

Both men were well aware of the way Hollywood normally treats historical advisors. Legendary Texas historians Lon Tinkle and J. Frank Dobie were invited by John Wayne to monitor his epic production of *The Alamo* in 1959. Both distinguished men soon resigned, furious and frustrated at being repeatedly ignored and patronized. The resulting film is a total work of fiction.

But if Hardin and Huffines expected similar treatment, they were to be surprised.

Hardin, author of the acclaimed *Texian Iliad: A Military History of the Texas Revolution,* says, "The thing I admire about these people from the costume designer to the set dressers to John Lee himself is that we always have these conversations. They don't always do what we suggest. But they always have a valid reason and we always have the conversation; they always hear us out.

The Historians
HARDIN AND HUFFINES

"This is not history," says Huffines, an active-duty military officer and author of *Blood of Noble Men: The Alamo Siege & Battle.* "This is Hollywood and everybody needs to understand that. But John Lee said that he never wants to make an artistic decision based on ignorance. He always wants to know the facts. For someone doing an historical epic it's so important to have that attitude."

Hancock says he was prepared for his relationship with the historians to be a rocky one. "At the start, of course," he says, "it's always a little difficult when the historians come in, because right off the bat, they all come in the same way, which is, 'You've got to do it this way or you're wrong!'" Hancock sent a copy of the script to Hardin and Huffines and asked them to go through it looking for inaccuracies or anachronisms. They found plenty of both, such as modern slang like "yeah" and "okay" which were not in use in 1836. The three men spent hours sifting through, correcting what could be corrected, and making peace with the rare instances when things were historically wrong but dramatically true.

Hancock says, "I told them right off the bat, 'I think the greatest sin is not to do it in an inaccurate way. The greatest sin is not knowing what accurate is.'"

And even though there were compromises to be made, neither historian finds much to complain about the way *The Alamo* turned out. "Just about everything you're gonna see happen in this film did happen," Huffines says. "What John Lee has done is rearrange some of the chronology so it fits the pace of the story a little better. He's a master writer and he's a master storyteller. He's getting at the truth of the Alamo and the Texas Revolution from his own perspective. It really is a privilege to work with somebody like that."

Hardin says, "I think they've never regretted that they hired us both because I think they need us both. I'm kind of the macro historian and Alan is the micro historian. I hope they feel that they got value from us and that we've been able to contribute in unique ways. But all these guys, they want to do this right. You want to help people like that. It's a privilege to help people who have really done their homework, who really have a passion for telling a story.

[Left] Cinematographer Dean Semler (right) sets up a shot from the Alamo walls.
[Upper-right] Historical advisors Alan C. Huffines (left) and Stephen L. Hardin, Ph.D., on the Bexar set.
[Right] Each facet of the Alamo church's design—down to the size and shape of the stones in its façade—was re-created perfectly. *[Photograph by Tammy Troglin]*

61

Arnaldo Carlos Vento

While Stephen L. Hardin and Alan C. Huffines helped the filmmakers attend to matters of historical accuracy and authenticity, another technical advisor was at work on *The Alamo* doing a job that few will notice. Arnaldo Carlos Vento is a novelist, professor, and historian who was hired to coach the Mexican characters to speak in the precise language of the period—which is notably different from current Spanish language styles.

"Officially they call me 'the dialect coach.'" Vento says. "But I'd like to think I do a little bit more than that. I took the job because of the challenge to be able to contribute not just in the area of language but in the areas of culture and history as well."

Language in the Mexico of 1836 was not only different from Spanish of today, it was further complicated by differences in social strata. "For example," Vento says, "We had a 'campesino de abuelo,' a farm worker who's plowing with some oxen. In that particular scene it was appropriate to get the actor to speak the dialect of the 'campesino,' which has a little sing-song to it.

THE CHALLENGES OF ARCHAIC SPANISH

"On the other hand," Vento continues, "we have Santa Anna, a very complex character. He is a tyrant sometimes, but sometimes very compassionate—he was unpredictable. I gave Santa Anna a more formal level of Spanish. And with respect to the generals that surround and that are under Santa Anna, it is important to use the old colonial expressions of respect. For example, 'vuestra excellencia.' We don't say that anymore. We say, 'su excellencia.' There are a number of others little linguistic markers of the time."

Although Vento, at the urging of the filmmakers, helped the actors speak in nineteenth-century idiom, he realized that, now and then, flexibility was needed for dramatic purposes. "I gave some leeway for modification by the major players," he says, "particularly Santa Anna and Castrillón because the actors have their own ideas about the character and the projection that they need to do. But it really did not modify the content. It's merely another way of expressing the same idea. So to that degree, the actors have made a contribution as well."

Vento says, "Language has so many variables, so many different ways to say the same thing. But the most important thing is to be culturally appropriate, not only for the character but for the times as well."

THE PSYCHOLOGY
OF STYLE
Costume Designer Daniel Orlandi

The popular image of the defenders of the Alamo is of rugged frontiersmen wearing fringed buckskin clothes and coonskin caps, their faces covered by long, shaggy beards. But in researching the Alamo, costume designer Daniel Orlandi discovered that the reality of 1836 was far different than most Alamo movies and paintings have led us to believe.

"Everyone has an idea of the styles at the Alamo," Orlandi says, "but since it happened in 1836, it came before chaps and cowboy hats and boots. Most of the men back then wore top hats and tailcoats, not chaps and spurs. What we perceive of as western wear did not come into vogue until later, say the 1840s and 1850s."

John Lee Hancock says he took to calling the look of *The Alamo*, "Dirty Dickens."

Because the men of the Alamo came from all walks of life, Orlandi had to make sure that their clothes—and the condition of their clothes—were both appropriate to the period and dramatically effective. "If somebody is a farmer and his wife made his jacket it's not going to be made of the best cloth," Orlandi says. "It's not going to be made with the same kind of construction as a lawyer's coat, which was made by a tailor in town. Sometimes I have to be more of a psychologist than anything, figuring out what each character would wear and how they would wear it and how old it would be. We wanted to be historically correct, but we want it to look real."

Even the colors of the clothing were carefully chosen to be both historically accurate and appropriate to the look of the film. Orlandi says, "Our defenders come from all walks of life but we are using a muted palette. In those days, clothes were colored with vegetable dyes, not chemical dyes, so you would have seen very little blue. In our costumes, there's a lot of warm earth tones, a lot of greens."

[Right] Costume Designer Daniel Orlandi (right) shares costume ideas with John Lee Hancock.

Hundreds of Mexican uniforms were created by artists from London to Hollywood to India.

"These uniforms are marvelous," says Emilio Echevarría, who portrays Mexican general Santa Anna. "You only have to put it on and now you don't have to do anything else but begin to act. They act by themselves, no?"

Over the nearly two years that Orlandi spent on the film, he dressed over 2,000 extras and 82 principal actors. Orlandi's crew supervised over 4,000 costumes, 1,000 Mexican shakos (tall military hats) and over 10,000 buttons.

To create the vast range of uniforms, dresses and street clothes, Orlandi drew upon sources from all over the world. The uniforms were made in Los Angeles. The shakos were made in India by a business that has made British uniforms for many decades. The intricate embroidery on the Mexican generals' uniforms and on the distinctive vest worn by David Crockett (Billy Bob Thornton) was all done by hand in Pakistan. Orlandi says, "They were one of the few places on earth that still does that kind of intricate, very precise hand gold

embroidery. The buttons were all molded for us from the original designs."

The Mexican uniforms of 1836 were modeled after Napoleonic uniforms and Orlandi and his crew replicated them perfectly. The ornate metal plate attached to the shakos was copied exactly from a genuine one found during an archeological dig at the Alamo in San Antonio.

In creating the clothing and uniforms for *The Alamo*, Orlandi aimed for the highest authenticity possible. But, he says, when all is said and done, the needs of the film are always more important than the demands of history.

"We can do most meticulous research," Orlandi says. "We can create the most beautiful, fantastic costumes. But if it's not helping the director tell his story then what's the point? If the audience is paying too much attention to what the characters are wearing, it takes away from the movie."

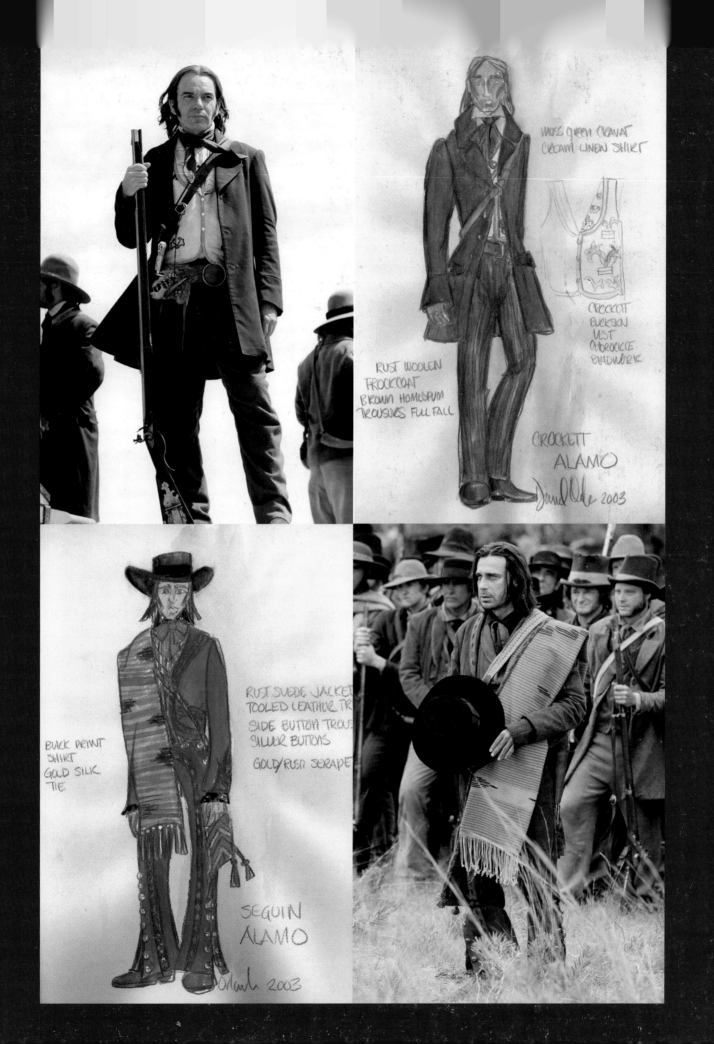

MOSS GREEN CRAVAT
CREAM LINEN SHIRT

CROCKETT
BUCKSKIN
VEST
CHEROKEE
BEADWORK

RUST WOOLEN
FROCKCOAT
BROWN HOMESPUN
TROUSERS FULL FALL

CROCKETT
ALAMO

David Cole 2003

BLACK PRINT
SHIRT
GOLD SILK
TIE

RUST SUEDE JACKET
TOOLED LEATHER TRIM
SIDE BUTTON TROUS
SILVER BUTTONS

GOLD/RUST SERAPE

SEGUIN
ALAMO

2003

Typically on a motion picture, the composer is the last artist hired. He or she normally waits for the film to be completed and then writes the score to the finished product.

But Carter Burwell signed onto *The Alamo* nearly from the beginning. John Lee Hancock says, "I knew that Carter was a guy that, when he takes a project, he cares a lot about it and is willing to work on it with you." Hancock knew that he was going to need several pieces of music written or arranged in advance for use in the film. He had the Disney music department scour their archives for period music, which they sent to the director. When he made his selections, he sent them on to Burwell.

Burwell is perhaps best known as the composer of the distinctive—sometimes quirky—scores for several films by the Coen Brothers—*Raising Arizona, Miller's Crossing, The Big Lebowski, O Brother, Where Art Thou?,* and others. Utilizing unusual orchestrations and experimental scoring techniques, Burwell has produced a body of work unlike that of any other composer in Hollywood.

He also produced a lovely score for John Lee Hancock's first film as director, *The Rookie*. "The thing I love about Carter is he's not going to throw bombastic at you," Hancock says. "I think there would be a real inclination on some composers' part to say, 'Wow, a big massive story. I get to go big—wall-to-wall!' I think that would be a mistake for *The Alamo*, because although you need the stuff that's rich and full and the 100-piece orchestra, you also need to be small and tender and 'less than.' Carter's really good at that, because you draw him into it."

"The other reason I wanted to use him," Hancock continues, "was because I felt very strongly about the Celtic influence that I wanted the music to follow, given the makeup of the Alamo garrison—Scots and Irishmen and Southerners. I think that his Irish lamentation in *Miller's Crossing* is so beautiful, and haunting. Like all good lamentations, it's joyful and sad at the same time. And I think that's what *The Alamo* is. It's the defeat that became a victory."

Burwell completed one piece about midway through filming, music for Davy Crockett that Burwell and Hancock informally referred to as "Fiddle Deguello."

"It's just so lovely," Hancock says. "I can't even imagine what it will be like with a ninety-piece orchestra playing—it's so haunting. It'll just be beautiful. I think that'll be one of the themes throughout. I just so enjoy working with Carter."

HAUNTING AND TENDER
COMPOSER CARTER BURWELL

MUSKETS AND LONG KNIVES
The Weaponry of the Alamo

The battle of the Alamo was fought with primitive weapons capable of inflicting powerful damage upon the enemy. The days of repeating rifles and revolvers were still in the future. The men of the Alamo and the Mexican army carried muzzle loaders, meaning that the ammunition had to be loaded through the barrel with the use of a ramrod. The firearms were capable of only one shot at a time. Experienced marksmen could reload in only a few seconds if the circumstances were right. But in the heat of battle, once that shot had been fired, the fighter was forced to turn to even more ancient means of ferocity—knives, bayonets, clubs, bare hands.

The task of finding—or re-creating—enough of these weapons to arm the hundreds of actors and extras in *The Alamo* fell to property master Don Miloyevich.

"These items are not available at the local convenience store," Miloyevich says. Of the 700 muskets used in the film, approximately half were rented and half were created just for *The Alamo*. Stock weapons houses carry large quantities of period weaponry for use in the film, but the relentless drive for authenticity in *The Alamo* led Miloyevich and his crew to cast a wider net. Some of the guns were manufactured in India and Italy. And various specialists around the country were called upon to build weapons specifically for the film.

Cannons Online, Inc., an artillery firm in Frederick, Maryland, manufactured fifteen Gribeauval six-pounders (cannon designed to fire six-pound balls), two 7" Howitzers, eight Garrison carriages, seven six-

pounder field carriages, two Field Howitzer carriages and one nine-pounder Congreve Volley Cart and limber (or tow cart). The carriages were made of solid mahogany—just like the originals.

Co-owner Chuck Tressler says that the impressive array of weaponry was produced in a mere fifty days—"a time period that included three major holidays, four snow days, and every weekend." The distinctive Congreve rocket launcher, cart, and limber, Tressler says, "are believed to be the first reproductions since they were first manufactured in the 1700s."

Adolphsen Bros. Custom Muzzleloading Firearms, located in South Hope, Maine, manufactured two Spanish holster pistols and two .62 calibre Spanish Catalan escopeta muskets.

"All of our guns are made from scratch and by hand," says Alan Adolphsen, "and that includes all metal parts, locks, and so on. They're made from black walnut, and all the metal is either steel or brass. It usually takes a couple of months to produce one gun. When we got the order from Disney to produce these guns for *The Alamo*, we had four weeks to do it. There were no reproduction parts available and there are only two of us!" Adolphsen laughs. "We specialize in 'unobtainium.'"

For the Mexican army equipment, Miloyevich says, he had to look a little farther afield. "The Mexican Army gear was made in China," he says, "because we could not get buff leather in North America. It's an old alkalide process and there's nothing that looks like it but that.

Many of the films' props are exact replicas of items on display at the real Alamo in San Antonio. Patrick Wilson wears a cat's eye ring that William Travis is said to have given to little Angelina Dickinson on the last day of the siege. "We copied Santa Anna's snuffbox," says Miloyevich, "as well as some of the jewelry dug up around the Alamo. We used that for the ladies that we saw at the fandango. The curator of the Alamo, Bruce Winders, was really very helpful. I thought I'd just go and breeze through the Alamo for a couple of hours, but we ended up spending the whole day there. He answered all our questions and explained the history of things. It was really very informative, and helped us a lot in the prep for this movie."

[Top left] Alan Adolphsen, of Adolphsen Bros. Custom Muzzleloading Firearms, holds three different stages of rifle stocks in the early stages.
[Left] Many intricate metal parts must be created and tooled in order to build a flintlock.

The Alamo was made on the largest standing set in North America. The production utilized hundreds of extras in meticulously tailored period costumes. Numerous weapons, all authentic to 1836, were created specifically for this film. In essence, an entire world from the past was re-created on a vast ranch in Texas. The aim was to make the experience of the siege and fall of the Alamo as accurate and authentic—as real—as possible. This is not a fantasy-based "special effects" movie.

And yet visual effects have been used with great skill and imagination to enhance the realism of The Alamo. Today, as visual effects technology continues to improve, filmmakers sometimes overuse those tools, creating massive battle scenes with thousands upon thousands of digitally created and animated extras. But Craig Barron, visual effects supervisor for Matte World Digital, which is in charge of The Alamo's visual effects, says that such an approach wouldn't be appropriate in this case.

"The visual effects in this movie are really decided by the style of the production," he says. "We're taking advantage of all the great resources that went into making the movie. It's been my approach to take what's there and enhance it. In fact, there were a lot of shots that might have been thought of traditionally as effects shots but the filmmakers were actually able to do them for real. Any visual effects person will tell you that if you can do it for real, it's always the best way to go."

A few dozen Mexican soldados (above) become, a vast army [left], marching through a freezing, rocky landscape—all courtesy of the artists at Matte World Digital.

Several dozen audience members were replicated to give this performance of "Lion of the West" a full house. The authentic limelights that line the stage were photographed separately and added digitally to the image.

The realistic look of *The Alamo* actually posed a challenge for Matte World Digital. The audience can easily detect an unnatural movement or an imperfect visual effect. "We have to make sure that our shots belong in the movie," Barron says. "If they're doing things practically with real soldiers firing weapons and people streaming over the walls and dynamic camera movement—all the things you want to do in a modern telling of the Alamo saga—the visual effects have to match that look."

Ironically, the better the artists at Matte World Digital do their job, the less detectable their work will be when the effects are cut into the finished motion picture. "That's our goal," Barron says.

One of Matte World Digital's primary tasks is "replication," or turning a few extras into many by photographing them several times and then combining all the groups into a single frame. The process sounds deceptively simple, but must be carefully planned and precisely executed.

For one scene showing the Mexican army marching toward Texas during a snowfall, not only were hundreds of extra soldiers added to the image through replication, but the snowflakes were added as well. And the landscape was turned from the low hills of Texas to a rocky mountain pass covered in snow—all through digital matte work.

In the scene when David Crockett (Billy Bob Thornton) attends the theater in Washington City (not yet D.C.), Barron's crew not only made the audience larger, but helped to take Austin's Paramount Theater on a journey through time.

Barron recalls, "We had 200 extras as theatergoers, which we replicated. They had to applaud and move around, from section to section. The finished scene looks like several hundred people enjoying the show."

Production Designer Michael Corenblith dressed the Paramount Theater to look appropriate to 1835. The stage was backed with a huge decorative curtain with scenes inspired by the legend of Davy Crockett. The film's technicians even managed to re-create the lovely but archaic style of stage lighting called limelight.

But it was then up to Matte World Digital's Chris Stoski to further erase signs of the twenty-first century from the Paramount. "Stoski had to take out all the Art Deco lighting fixtures," says Craig Barron. "And the theater was actually a little too big so he made it smaller by putting a digital wall behind the balcony." He laughs. "And, of course, Stoski had to digitally remove the 'Exit' signs and the wheelchair ramps—all things that they wouldn't have known about in 1835."

One of the most beautiful—and terrifying—shots in the film is what the artists at Matte World Digital call the "final siege." It depicts the last moments of the battle as the Mexican army stream over the walls of the Alamo and into the courtyard—all seen from above, with the entire Alamo compound within the frame.

Barron says, "The idea of the shot came from John Lee Hancock. He noticed that in many books about the Alamo, you often see a God's-eye view of the battle. John said it would be great to do a visual effects shot like that."

Production designer Michael Corenblith gave his set drawings to Barron, who digitized them to create, he says, "a little CG model, not textured to realism, but sort of like an architectural model. Then we could move our camera around and choose the best angle to shoot this scene from."

They decided to place the camera on a crane, 100 feet in the air, manned by camera operator Patrick Loungeway, who was equipped with a VistaVision special effects camera and a walkie-talkie. Cinematographer Dean Semler lit the scene for battle and then assistant director K. C. Hodenfield began instructing the Mexican army where and when to attack.

"We divided the shot sort of like slicing a pie," Barron says. "We would have troops attack and scale the walls and then stream into the courtyard. Then we would move them around and have them do it again. After they did the north wall, they would do the south wall, then the west wall…

"This way," he continues, "we built a shot that was comprised of many different elements. There are also flares flying overhead that illuminate the Alamo and the troops. So there's interactive lighting that's happening during the scene. And the straw roofs are catching on fire, so we would shoot those separately as well. You can see the shadows of the soldiers as they run past the Alamo church. Then, back at the studio, Paul Rivera, our chief digital compositor, built this layered image composed of all these elements. We added a slight camera move on it also, so that it feels like we're getting a little bit closer to the fort while the attack is happening, to give it even more dramatic impact."

Barron says, "It's a really fabulous shot and we're very excited about it. It's quite overwhelming—it reads very clearly that this is the end of the battle of the Alamo."

Although Barron and his Matte World Digital artists can create entire worlds out of 0s and 1s in the computer, he says that he was particularly impressed with the sense of realism on *The Alamo* set.

"Often when you're on a set or on a location," Barron says, "the camera is pointing at what you're shooting, if you look around, the illusion is ruined—you'll be in the middle of a modern city, or the set will be unfinished or you'll be on a soundstage. What was really striking about immersing yourself in this world that was created for *The Alamo* is that so much of it was created for the film all around you. If you look in another direction, there's defenders walking around, or Bexar townspeople all dressed up like 1836. It's like having traveled in a time machine to see and place and time that doesn't exist anymore. It's really a tremendous amount of fun to work on this film, and it's rare to be able to say that. Everybody on *The Alamo* knows they're working on something special and that comes across."

[Overleaf] A stunning overhead shot of the final moments of the battle consists of many different images filmed on the set, then digitally combined by Matte World Digital.

REMEMBER THE ALAMO

In the weeks following the fall of the Alamo, Sam Houston led his army east, accompanied much of the way by terror-stricken settlers, fleeing back to the safety of the United States. It was known as the "Runaway Scrape."

Historians continue to debate whether Houston was similarly running for his life, Santa Anna hot on his trail, or cleverly leading the Mexican army along, looking for just the perfect spot to stop and fight.

Although that argument may never be settled, what happened on April 21, 1836 is beyond dispute.

The armies of Santa Anna and General Cos joined at a marshy place near what is now Houston, Texas. Their backs were up against a body of water called Peggy's Lake. There was no road out of the area except by a single bridge. Yet he was so confident after the victories at the Alamo and at Goliad that Santa Anna saw no reason to fear the outnumbered Texians under Houston. Nevertheless, the Mexicans built barricades to prepare for battle, should it come.

But it didn't.

For hour after hour, all day, through the night and

well into the next day, the Mexicans stood guard, knowing that Houston's army was only a few hundred yards away. As the time wore wearily on, the soldados' vigilance began to relax. Some of the men dropped in exhaustion and went to sleep. Santa Anna himself was resting in his tent.

At about four P.M., Houston knew it was time to attack. He had no buglers, so he enlisted the aid of a drummer and two fifers. They didn't know any military charges—in fact, the only tune they all knew was a slightly bawdy love song called "Come to the Bower." So that's what they played.

Houston led his men across the field. Some of them shouted "Remember the Alamo!" Others called out "Remember Goliad." They swept over the Mexican battlements in a frenzy of bloodlust and vengeance. The battle lasted only 18 minutes but in that time the Texians slaughtered nearly 650 Mexicans and captured 700 more. Santa Anna fled for his life, but was soon captured, as was General Cos. General Castrillón died bravely in battle, his arms folded calmly over his chest when he ran out of ammunition.

The Battle of San Jacinto is the action that won Texas its independence from Mexico—and it is the climax of *The Alamo*, the moment when defeat turned into victory.

Needless to say, filming the battle took longer than eighteen minutes. In fact, it took nearly as many days.

A beautiful location was found near Batrop, Texas, on an 840-acre ranch which offered forest, an open field, and a lake. Historical advisor Stephen L. Hardin, Ph.D., says, "It was a lot dustier than the real place would have been—after all, San Jacinto was a swamp. But this looks great on camera."

A few hundred extras and reenactors gathered to portray the Texians. A great many of them simply made camp a few hundred yards from the set, living life as it might have been in 1836—with a few improvements.

Larry Grimsley, one of the reenactors, says, "We had hot showers, a kitchen, electricity, porta-potties that were serviced daily, a big tent with snacks, and a television. When we were finished with the day's scheduled shooting there was always something hot to eat, sandwiches, chicken fried steaks, etc. The production company had plenty of food for us during breakfast and lunch. Tents were also air conditioned."

John Lee Hancock had determined that the battle

would be as authentic as possible. Historical advisors Stephen Hardin and Alan C. Huffines helped out with something more than just dry facts—something a little more high-tech: "We choreographed the battle on Powerpoint and animated it," Huffines says.

"We did it historically accurate—no Hollywood play in it, nothing like that. It's a way of telling John Lee, 'This is exactly what they did at this piece of ground and over here they did this.' He's a very visual person. So rather than me telling him what happened, he can look at it and decide what to use and what not to use for his film."

The real battle took only eighteen minutes but filming it took day after exhausting day, often in sweltering heat.

"On that first day," says reenactor Jerry Laing, "they had us charging the soldado encampment from as far away as the opposite tree line—at least the length of a football field. We did about six or seven takes from various distances on record hot days—114 degrees, I'm told—over very uneven, dusty ground."

Ned Huthmacher, a California-based reenactor, remembers attacking again and again in the hot sun. "Dennis Quaid had us jumping to his orders to fire and advance across the broken, dusty ground," he says. "Water trucks came by every so often to spray down the dry earth and grass [to minimize the dust]. The oppressive heat had us Texian boys gulping down the liquid refreshments as often as possible, with numerous visits to the woods and Mister Tree."

But even though the massive movement of troops,

with cannon and musket fire, horse falls and stunts took on the mammoth proportions of a logistical nightmare, director John Lee Hancock always had to keep in mind the subtler demands of story and character.

He says, "I had completely forgotten about Manuel Castrillón's death, crossing his arms. I'd even written it in the script, and I'd read through it again, but here we were, and it was 102 degrees, and you're trying to do this, that, and the other, and block stuff out. And Steve Hardin reminded me of the crossed arms. I said, 'Oh, boy, thank you.' Because here I was in the heat of all this million things going on, and I was going to drop the ball."

Hancock continues, "Also, I had wanted somebody to die in Peggy's Lake with an underwater shot coming toward us, to kind of get us out of the battle of San Jacinto to Santa Anna's capture. Steve Hardin and Alan Huffines said, 'Well, you know, [Santa Anna's aide] Batres died in Peggy's Lake.' I said, 'Thank you! Perfect!'"

Even though the heat was sometimes unbearable and the work exhausting, Hancock says he was always struck by how deeply affected everyone was about the story they were telling. He says, "I just can't tell you how many times a day an extra would come up and say, 'Thank you.' And I would say, of course, 'Thank you.' So many of these people had a relative who had fought at the Alamo or San Jacinto. And sometimes it was just somebody from Texas, who had devoted his life to the subject. They'd say to me, 'Gosh, I'll remember this the rest of my life. I have something to tell my grandkids.'"

THE SCREENPLAY

Written by Leslie Bohem and Stephen Gaghan and John Lee Hancock

FADE IN:

THE BLACK SCREEN BECOMES WAFTING BLACK SMOKE. We're in—

INT. ALAMO COURTYARD—DAY

But we can't really tell because we don't see much of the architecture—*shots interrupted and connected by smoke.* We see too much and not enough at the same time:

• A MUTT DOG, completely out of sorts, licks A TEXIAN'S dead face (Tom Waters)—urging his master to come to life. A MEXICAN SOLDIER drags a body toward the pyre, WIPING FRAME.

• A MEXICAN SOLDIER (ESPARZA) holds the dead body of his brother GREGORIO (a Texian) and MOANS as he carries him away.

• TWO TEJANO WOMEN cover their noses with cloths and cross themselves.

• JAMES BONHAM is dragged to a funeral pyre.

• A Mexican soldier—gut-shot and dying—mumbles a prayer.

• A pair of BROKEN GLASSES lie beside a dead hand.

• A dead Mexican soldier—JOSE TORRES—lies draped against the flag pole.

• Scratched on the top of a wall—13 marks.

We're seeing the aftermath of the final assault of the Alamo. *And then something we didn't expect to see—*

• A haunting still life of death. A man lies on his back, his dead eyes staring right through us. DAVID CROCKETT.

• Another still life—a man lies in bed, one arm draped over the side—a bloody wall behind his head. JAMES BOWIE.

• And then—a man on his back, his eyes facing the noon sun. WILLIAM BARRET TRAVIS. As he's dragged OUT OF FRAME...

• As bodies are dragged from the long barracks TWO MEXICAN OFFICERS eye the proceedings with some evident distaste.

ALMONTE (Spanish)
A great victory, no?

CASTRILLÓN (Spanish)
Another such victory and we'll all go to the devil.

As black smoke from burning bodies fills the frame—

In 1821 Mexico won independence from Spain and with it the vast land holdings which included the northernmost state of Coahuila y Tejas.

In an attempt to further colonize this territory and help stave off marauding Indians, Anglos were granted land and tax advantage to move to the state. And they came. So many in fact that Antonio López de Santa Anna, Mexico's elected President turned Dictator, closed the borders and sent occupational troops into the state.

In an effort to enforce their rights as citizens of Mexico or form their own republic, the citizens of Tejas—Anglo and Tejano—began to organize a provisional government.

And to prepare for war.

The smoke...

One year ago.

becomes CIGAR SMOKE wafting in front of camera as A MAN passes. When it clears we see SAM HOUSTON—

EXT. THEATRE—WASHINGTON, D.C.—NIGHT

—standing near a theatre, watching PLAYGOERS make their way to a performance.

HOUSTON
(mumbling to himself)
Take the oath of militia duty and you will receive 640 acres...640 acres...Of your choosing....

He takes a swig from a flask, eyes the night and continues mumbling...

HOUSTON (cont'd)
Invest now...Invest now or...
Lament later.

Satisfied with his spiel, he stumbles toward the theatre entrance.

INT. D.C. THEATRE—BACKSTAGE—DRESSING ROOM—NIGHT

HACKETT (O.S.)
I'm a screamer. I got the roughest racin' horse, the prettiest sister, the surest rifle and the ugliest dog in the district.

PAN ACROSS a wall with handbills—"JAMES HACKETT in LION OF THE WEST." We land on the ACTOR'S FACE—

over-adorned in beaver cap and wilderness duds as he runs lines in a mirror.

HACKETT (cont'd)
My old man can lick anybody in Tennessee and I can lick my old man. I can outgrin a panther and ride a lightnin' bolt, tote a steamboat on my back and whip my weight in wildcats. I'm half horse and half alligator with a whiff of harricane throwed into the bargain!

A KNOCK. The door opens and the STAGE MANAGER appears.

HACKETT (cont'd)
What? What is it?!

STAGE MANAGER
He's here.

HACKETT
(perturbed, turns)
Who's here?

STAGE MANAGER
He's here.

Off the shock on Hackett's face—

INT. THEATRE—NIGHT

Packed. All heads turn at a grand entrance in a box above. DAVID CROCKETT, fully aware of the stir he's causing, smiles as he takes his seat with a few DISTINGUISHED FELLOWS in tow.

IN THE WINGS

Hackett, sweating bullets, watches, mumbles to himself...

HACKETT
Just another performance. Just another—

The curtain opens and the audience APPLAUDS. Hackett, no longer able to hide, covers with a smile and steps forward. He looks out into the clapping audience until his eyes find—

CROCKETT—smiling and clapping with a bit of a "show me" look on his face. Everyone in the place is eyeing Crockett's reaction. When the applause dies...

Hackett takes a baby step forward and still sweating...

HACKETT (cont'd)
Before we, uh, begin tonight's... performance, I should like to acknowledge the presence of the man whose...life... "inspired" this humble play.

(bows to Crockett)
Good evening, Mr. Crockett.

Everyone in the place watches, waits. Crockett slowly stands, faces off with Hackett. Then bows himself...

CROCKETT
Good evening, Mr. Crockett.

Tension broken. To more wild applause—

ICE cracked by icepick. HAND starts to put some in a glass.

HOUSTON (V.O.)
Keep your ice.

INT. BALLROOM /BAR—NIGHT

SAM HOUSTON grabs his drink from the nearby bar and turns back to entertaining TWO WELL-DRESSED BUSINESSMEN, SMITH and JONES. Houston is trying a bit too hard....

HOUSTON
If it doesn't burn going down how can you be sure it's bad for you? I'll be interested to see you gentlemen when you arrive in Texas and have your first taste of mescal.

Houston downs the drink in one slow, steady pull.

MR. SMITH
Is it the truth that men and women imbathe together, in the open?

HOUSTON
Cleanliness is next to godliness.

MR. JONES
How godly can a place be if Jim Bowie calls it home?

HOUSTON
Jim married into a fine Tejano family, found out you don't have to skirt the law to get rich in Texas.

IN ANOTHER PART OF THE ROOM

Crockett holds court to a group of men while Hackett, grinning, no longer sweating, stands alongside.

CROCKETT
More me than I am myself. I have half a mind to hire Mr. Hackett here to play me seven days a week—I would dearly love some time away. Of course the citizens of Tennessee may grant me that wish come next election.

Laughs. Crockett notices Houston across the room, excuses himself, shakes a few more hands on the way over...

MR. SMITH
What say the Mexicans of all this? I mean, is the Mexican army not occupying San Antonio de Bexar as we speak?

HOUSTON
For now.

Not the answer they wanted to hear. As they wander off...

HOUSTON (cont'd)
Invest now gentlemen. Or lament later.

CROCKETT
Sam Houston. Making friends wherever you go.
(off Houston's glance)
Enjoy the performance?

HOUSTON
From the day I met you.

Houston moves to the bar, accepts a refill.

CROCKETT
(raises his glass)
To Tennessee.

HOUSTON
To hell with Tennessee, David.
(looks up; raises glass)
To Texas.

CROCKETT
You'll turn on an old girl quick, won't you, Sam?

HOUSTON
Wait until she turns on you.
(a beat)
What you deserve for defending Indians.

CROCKETT
Least I'll earn the honor of being dis-elected.
(a sore spot)
Beg your pardon, Governor.

SMITH AND JONES

Off to the side, watching...

MR. SMITH
Sad, isn't it? A year ago we'd be looking upon two men with their caps set for the White House. Now?...

HOUSTON AND CROCKETT

CROCKETT
What are you peddling?

HOUSTON
Something a certain congressman might need before long.

CROCKETT
You selling rocking chairs?

HOUSTON
I'm selling Texas.

CROCKETT
What would I want with Norte Mexico?

HOUSTON
Texas. No man will invest in a war to remain a province of Mexico.

CROCKETT
You figger on becoming part of the U.S.?

HOUSTON
(smiles, raises glass)
To the Republic of Texas.

Crockett reluctantly toasts and drinks.

HOUSTON (cont'd)
Remember how Tennessee was?
(off Crockett's look)
Better. Timber, water, game, cattle, and more land than you have ever seen. Take the oath for militia duty and you will receive 640 acres of your choosing.

CROCKETT
(intrigued)
Of my choosing...

As Crockett considers, Houston spots a MAN IN A SUIT in the middle of the room.

HOUSTON
Now that man looks to have capital.

He pats Crockett's shoulder and walks away.

CROCKETT
Sam?!
(Houston stops; turns)
You figger this new Republic is gonna need a President?

Crockett and Houston share a look and a smile.

EXT. BEXAR—SUPER: SAN ANTONIO DE BEXAR—DAY

As the San Fernando church bell RINGS we see a processional of defeated MEXICAN TROOPS file out of the west end of town. JUAN SEGUIN, noble, sits on his horse, watching. DON JOSE PALAEZ, is alongside in a horse drawn cart.

          PALAEZ (Spanish)
     Will they return?

          SEGUIN (Spanish)
     No. General Cos gave his word.

          PALAEZ (Spanish)
     When I heard that the Mexicans surrendered, I didn't believe it. How did the bastards accomplish this?

          SEGUIN (Spanish)
     With *our* hearts.

AT THE EDGE OF TOWN

Several TEXIANS, most prominently THE NEW ORLEANS GREYS watch as they go, chiding them.

          GREY #1
     Loosianna just whipped your arse! Kentucky just whipped your arse! Tennessee just whipped your arse!
          (to his pal)
     Santanna sends 'em here, we send 'em back!

          GREY #2
     Yer lucky we let you keep your muskets. Should just let the savages swallow you whole!

          GREY #1
     Now scat and don't come back!

Grey #1 spits in the direction of—GENERAL MARTIN COS, who hesitates for a moment, stares at the two men, trying to retain some pride, then rides by.

EXT. A SMALL TOWN—SUPER: SAN FELIPE DE AUSTIN—DAY

Wood frame houses line the one main street. There is a reasonable amount of bustle to this place—people walking, talking, men on horses, wagons loading, etc.

          TRAVIS (V.O.)
     You marked the coat as swallow tail?

INT. INGRAM'S GENERAL STORE/BARROOM—DAY

In the front—foodstuffs, tobacco, Mexican blankets, gourds, guns, saddles. In the back, a barroom with rickety tables and excess provisions. WILLIAM TRAVIS leans over the counter, spelling out the particulars of a hand-written sales order.

          MR. INGRAM
     As you desired, Mr. Travis.

          TRAVIS
     Lt. Colonel.
          (off Owner's look)
     And the piping as onyx?

Travis points to A SKETCH of a man in the exact uniform he's ordering. The drawn man looks a lot like Travis.

          MR. INGRAM
     Should be quite a sight. Where would you like the uniform sent?

Travis isn't quite sure how to take this.

          TRAVIS
     San Antonio de Bexar. I'll be posted there. To defend the town.

          MR. INGRAM
     Defend against what? Mexican army left Bexar with their tails between their legs.

          JOE (O.S.)
     Mister William?

Travis turns to see his slave, JOE, 25, standing in the door.

          JOE (cont'd)
     She here. In yer office. Waitin'.
          (off Travis's look)
     Yer wife.

EXT. A DOG TROT—DAY

CU—JAMES BOWIE—through a barred window. He looks like hell, trying hard to concentrate on something. In the background WE SEE Bowie's slave SAM, 40, at the entrance to the street.

          SAM
     Mister James?...

Bowie has a coughing fit, throws up. We NOW SEE that Bowie is drunk, puking against a wall, with Sam keeping watch.

A group of RIDERS race down the street behind Sam. Bowie straightens himself and hurries toward the street.

EXT. MAIN STREET—DAY

Travis walks down the street with Joe in tow. Bowie ambles in the opposite direction, headed somewhere with purpose. Men in the street gladhand him. As Bowie and Travis pass—

          TRAVIS
     Colonel.

          BOWIE
     Buck.

Their slaves, Joe and Sam, share a look that gives a hint of the relationship, or lack thereof, between their owners. After Travis and Bowie are out of ear-shot of one another.

          TRAVIS
     Drunken Hottentot.

          BOWIE
     Two-bit swell.

Bowie buttonholes one of the dismounted riders, DEAF SMITH—

          BOWIE (cont'd)
     Deaf! Deaf, you come from Bexar?

          DEAF SMITH
     Ain't it so.

          BOWIE
     How's my home?

          DEAF SMITH
     Free of the Mexican army. Fought 'em straight into the old mission, then right out again.

          BOWIE
     Is it wrecked bad? The house?!

Deaf hesitates, choosing his words carefully.

          DEAF SMITH
     There was quite a bit of cannon shot, Jim.

Off Bowie's concern—

INT. LAW OFFICE—DAY

A tow-headed CHILD of seven stares... at Travis. A sad woman, ROSANNA TRAVIS, urges him forward.

          ROSANNA
     Go on, Charlie. You remember him. Don't you remember your father?

TRAVIS
(holds hand up)
When I last saw you, you were *this* tall.

Nothing from the boy. Travis looks at the little girl, three, who also shyly stares.

TRAVIS *(cont'd)*
What are you calling her? Lizzy? Betsy?

Travis tries to approach the little girl.

ROSANNA
Elisabeth.

The little girl shies away from him. He turns to some papers on the desk.

TRAVIS
The choices are abandonment, adultery, or cruel and barbarous treatment. I think abandonment's the most accurate.

ROSANNA
Last time I saw you, you were lying in bed next to me. Then I closed my eyes. That was four years ago.
(re: the document)
Any of the choices would be appropriate.

TRAVIS
That's true, Rosanna. That's certainly true.

Travis solemnly signs the document. He watches Rosanna do the same. She puts the papers in her bag.

ROSANNA
Are you sure you want to do this?

TRAVIS
We've signed the papers.

ROSANNA
I meant Charlie.

TRAVIS
I don't intend this harshly, but he should have manly example in his life.
(off her look)
I've already made arrangements for him to stay with a fine family while I'm away.
(she nods; after a beat)
They promoted me to lieutenant colonel. Did I tell you that in the letter?

ROSANNA
I can't say I'm happy for you, Billy.
(beat)
Well... we have a long way to travel.

Rosanna kneels down and gives the boy a long hug.

ROSANNA (CONT'D)
Your father's becoming a rich man and he'll be able to see to your education.

Rosanna stands, looks at her son one last time, then takes Elisabeth's hand and leaves the law office. Elisabeth steals one look at her father as the door closes. Travis just stares for a moment, then turns to Charlie and trades a look with the confused young boy.

TRAVIS
We have a tutor...to learn you Spanish... Hola, Carlos. That means hello, Charlie.

Travis glances through the window—his wife and daughter walk away forever.

INT. PUBLIC BUILDING—DAY

A low-ceilinged place with unpainted boards. It's standing room only.

The room is divided into the PEACE PARTY and the WAR PARTY. There is T.J. RUSK, an able man, GOVERNOR HENRY SMITH, shrill and angry. JAMES GRANT, MOSELY BAKER, rash, ignorant men, and DAVID BURNET, who neither swears nor drinks, but carries a bible in one pocket, a gun in the other.

GRANT
You wanna call me an opportunist? Hell yes, I'm an opportunist. Taking Bexar changes everything. We're in control now!

GOVERNOR SMITH
We swore allegiance to Mexico under the Federalist constitution of 1824—

As Mosely Baker interrupts his veins are popping with anger.

MOSELY BAKER
Santa Anna tore that document up personally, did he not, and named himself supreme dictator. The Centralists have changed the rules and I for one ain't swearing

allegiance to no son-of-a-bitch dictator.

Table slapping, knuckle rolling and shouts of "HEAR, HEAR."

GOVERNOR SMITH
Gentlemen, are we fighting for restoration of the Mexican Constitution of 1824 or for independence from Mexico?

Half the room yells INDEPENDENCE, the others CONSTITUTION. JUAN SEGUIN, Tejano leader, takes the floor.

JUAN SEGUIN
We can oppose the dictator Santa Anna, *but as loyal Mexicans.* Every man in this room became a Catholic and a Mexican citizen in order to immigrate here. Sam Houston is general of the army—

GRANT
Sir, he is NOT the general of the men who tasted victory at Bexar!

BURNET
And where is Houston, Senor Seguin? Where is the good general—?

AN EMPTY SHOT GLASS hits the table. We're—

INT. INGRAM'S GENERAL STORE/BARROOM—DAY

Sam Houston, alone, starts to pour another shot. His hand shakes. He sets down the bottle, prepares for another try.

MATHEW INGRAM, 15, sweeps in the main room, notices Houston's palsy, then cuts his eyes when Houston catches his stare. Mathew's father carries supplies into the bar.

INGRAM
Are you all right?

HOUSTON
I've about returned to ought, which is a fairly good starting point, actually.
(reaches for bottle again)
Obliged to you for asking.

Juan Sequin enters the barroom—

SEGUIN (English)
Time to go, General.

Houston ignores Seguin, concentrating as he pours from the bottle, making sure Mathew notices the steadiness of his hand. Then he throws back the shot.

HOUSTON
Drunk back sober is a miracle of the first order.

SEGUIN (English)
General?...

Houston rises, tosses a coin on the table. As it settles—

ON THE COIN is a military leader and the words General Antonio López de Santa Anna.

EXT. SAN FELIPE—DAY

As Houston and Seguin walk down the street, Houston seems to fill with the fresh air, his posture and demeanor changing with each step. Every man who sees him watches him pass.

HOUSTON
Matamoros? Why in the hell they want to capture Matamoros?

SEGUIN
They want to loot the port. They have the taste of blood in their mouths.

HOUSTON
They'll lose their fire once they realize it's their own.

At that moment, Travis, followed by Joe (who carries saddlebags), falls in with Houston and Seguin.

TRAVIS
General Houston, might you spare me a moment?

Houston pauses, looks at Travis.

TRAVIS (cont'd)
Sir, would you reconsider my posting to Bexar? Now that's it's been taken back... It's just... I'm a cavalry officer, sir, and my abilities would be better employed outside of a town and old mission.

Travis nods to Joe who opens the saddlebag. Travis pulls the uniform sketch and shows it to Houston.

TRAVIS (cont'd)
Sir, I have proposed a legion of cavalry—

HOUSTON
Place it in writing—

TRAVIS
I've already done so, Sir.

Joe pulls a packet of papers that he passes to Travis. He offers them to Houston, who doesn't take them.

HOUSTON
You're a lawyer, Travis? Are you not?

TRAVIS
Yes, I am. As you are, Sir.

Travis looks at Houston expectantly.

HOUSTON
Well, God is surely smiling on Texas.

Travis stops, realizing he's being patronized. Houston and Seguin continue on...

HOUSTON (cont'd)
Explain to me why young men measure themselves with fights instead of yardsticks?

SEGUIN
Why are you so hard on him?

HOUSTON
Reminds me of me.

EXT. SAN FELIPE—DAY (CONTINUOUS)

Houston and Juan walk toward the crowd gathered outside the Public Building.

SEGUIN
They're going to want you a bit humble, General.

Houston lets this sink in, hesitating. The crowd stares.

HOUSTON
I humble myself before God and there the list ends.

The crowd parts to let them through.

INT. PUBLIC BUILDING—DAY

More chaos with the men huddled in groups, working over documents. Burnet stalks the room, seemingly in control.

BURNET
The question has come to the floor whether to capture Matamoros—

Burnet sees Houston walk in and lean against a wall.

BURNET (cont'd)
Discussion on the point which is whether to capture Matamoros.

Burnet points to Grant who stands and gestures toward a large tactical map of Texas y Coahuila tacked on the wall.

GRANT
By attacking Matamoros we guarantee Texas independence. We hurl the thunder back in the very atmosphere of the enemy, dragging him and with him, the war, out of Texas.

GOVERNOR SMITH
Well, we can certainly guess who has land holdings in the Mexican interior...
(beat)
Now worthless.

MEN in the room make HISSING sounds.

GOVERNOR SMITH
(cont'd)
This whole council is more corrupt than perdition. In war, when spoils are the object, friends and enemies share a common destiny—

MOSELY BAKER
Spoils? We're talking about guts. About having enough of them to finish the task!

Rabid CHEERS from most of the room. Houston looks around, shaking his head. Then he slowly starts to walk around the room. Eyes slowly go to him.

HOUSTON
No leadership. No training. Few supplies. Less ammunition.

He arrives at the map, pulls a sabre from one of the men, sticks the tip to a point on the map.

HOUSTON (cont'd)
To march an expedition from here—to Matamoros—
(cuts the map to Matamoros)
Is lunacy. You do not split an army into vagabond militias that march off on the slightest pretext like bloodthirsty rabble.

He tosses the sabre on the table and continues his walk.

HOUSTON (cont'd)
Do you really believe this war is over? It has not even begun and already the scoundrels are rushing off for personal gain.

Houston expects approbation, instead there is SILENCE, then slowly come MURMURS of "COWARD," "QUITTER," "DRUNK," and "YELLOW." The TAUNTS grow LOUDER. Houston becomes arrogant.

HOUSTON (cont'd)
All new lands are infested by noisy, second-rate men who favor the rash and extreme measure.
(taking in the room)
Texas, quite obviously, is overrun with them.

The men are now openly against him.

BURNET
You opposed taking Bexar where victory was ours. Now, you oppose Matamoros where victory will be as sweet. Perhaps, sir, you simply oppose fighting?

The men erupt in agreement.

MOSELY BAKER
Fighters shall lead the new country of Texas!

BURNET
The council will now consider the removal of General Houston from command of the regular army. All in favor... A show of hands?

The majority of the room erupts with raised arms and "hear, hear..." We see T.J. Rusk hesitate, then raise his hand.

GOVERNOR SMITH
(to Burnet)
You, Sir, do not speak for Texas. I'm governor and I hereby dissolve the council.

BURNET
All in favor of impeaching Governor Smith?!

Another ROUSING CHEER and show of hands. Red, pinched faces, shouting, "MATAMOROS," "VICTORY," "GOD BLESS TEXAS." Houston's voice is futile against the mob.

HOUSTON
The militias must report to the general of the army. We must have unity of command—

BURNET
To whom the militias report is no longer any of your concern. The regular army shall report to Colonel James Fannin, a West Point attendee.

JAMES FANNIN, West Point poster-boy, steps forward to raucous backslapping. The men are already leaving to fight.

HOUSTON
Amateur soldiers in the service of amateur politicians...

GRANT
The late, great Sam Houston. Former governor of Tennessee, former general of the Texian army—

HOUSTON
The fighting at Bexar has obviously produced chaos. The next will result in annihilation—

GRANT
Coward!

HOUSTON
Scottish catamite!

GRANT
What did you say?

HOUSTON
I called you a Scottish catamite, Grant—one step down from associate pederast—

Grant draws his knife. Houston rips open his shirt and bares his chest—

HOUSTON (cont'd)
Come for me!—

Seguin sighs and steps in behind Houston. Grant is about to take a step forward, when all heads around him turn.

Jim Bowie, just inside the door, smiling.

BOWIE
Any excuse to remove your clothes, right, Houston?

GRANT
This ain't your concern, Mr. Bowie.

HOUSTON
Indeed...
(Scotch, mimicking Grant)
This is between me and the catamite—

Grant flinches. Bowie puts a hand on his hip, letting his jacket slide open enough to expose a KNIFE sheathed to his side. Everyone in the room knows the legend of that knife. Bowie tenders it to Grant, handle first.

BOWIE
You want to borrow mine, Grant?
(right at Grant)
Because I will surely *give it to you.*

Everyone in the room stares back and forth between Bowie and Grant. Bowie

sets the knife on the table near Grant—"go for it." After a pregnant beat, Grant re-sheaths his knife. Bowie walks over and rebuttons Houston's shirt—showing his back to Grant, who stares down at the knife in front of him but dares not do anything about it.

BOWIE (cont'd)
You gentlemen will have to excuse Sam. He was Indian raised.

Bowie puts an arm around Houston and they walk out. Bowie "remembers" his knife, returns for it and slowly drags it across the table. Everyone watches; no one breathes.

EXT. SAN FELIPE STREET—NIGHT

MILITIA saddles up and rides out, HOOTING, certain of victory. Grant among them.

Bowie watches them leave, shakes his head, then walks away—passing a dog trot—the one in which we met Bowie. He stops—did he hear something?—looks down the alley.

A figure sits at the end, against the back wall, lit from windows on either side of the dog trot.

EXT. END OF THE ALLEY—NIGHT

Sam Houston sits splayed on the ground, head resting against the wall. Eyes closed. Drunk. In one hand is an almost empty bottle, in the other a pistol.

HOUSTON
Pull up a stool.

Bowie looks up, spots the barred window and remembers that only a few hours before, this exact spot was where he had vomited. He decides to squat.

BOWIE
Oblige me and don't sleep here tonight.

Houston takes a long pull on the bottle.

BOWIE (cont'd)
You're making a jackass of yourself, Sam.

HOUSTON
Vindictive sons-a-bitches. Sent me off to make treaty with the Cherokees.

Houston passes the bottle to Bowie. Bowie takes a swig.

BOWIE

You're going home. I slept on rocks outside of Bexar for three months while that paper-collared brother-in-law of Santa Anna's lived in my home, drinking up all my liquor. Everything I had is gone. Everything on paper any-ways.

Houston stares out into the darkness.

HOUSTON
(speechifying)
Texas was a chance, a second chance, for all of us. A place to wash away our sins. That means something. Don't ever forget it.

Bowie looks sideways at Houston who takes the bottle and punctuates his point with another swig of whiskey.

HOUSTON (cont'd)
Texas is wasted on the Texians.

BOWIE
The land's too good for the people.

HOUSTON
You can't blame the land.
(a beat)
They'll be back. The Mexicans, a massive well-trained army. Against a handful of amateurs. Only chance we have is to fight them in the open. Washington—fox and hound. 1812. Indian wars. Keep moving; burn what you leave behind. Forts are use-less to us.
(a beat)
What is it about that damnable place?

BOWIE
What place?

HOUSTON
Alamo. Whenever the wind blows sour in Bexar everybody runs there and hides. Nothing but mud and a caved-in church.

BOWIE
And cannon. It protects my home, Sam.

HOUSTON
You don't have a home. Any more than I do.

We can see this hurts Bowie a bit. Hous-ton sees it, too.

HOUSTON (cont'd)
It's a damn shame about your wife, Jim.

BOWIE
Damn shame about yours, too, Sam.

A moment—two men with not much left. Then Houston regains his fire, looks right at Bowie.

HOUSTON
Am I your general?

BOWIE
You know you are.

HOUSTON
I want you to return to Bexar, blow up the Alamo, and fetch back the cannon. Promise me you'll do this?

Bowie considers, then nods.

EXT. THE STREET OF SAN FELIPE—DAY

A bright clear day, cool, overexposed. The street is quiet and empty, as if things are back to normal and the town is again fragile. Hogs root in the road for some-thing to eat.

Houston, looking worse in the light of day, finishes cinching his huge white horse, then wipes his cotton mouth and mounts.

MATHEW
General?...

Mathew stands in the street alongside Houston.

MATHEW (cont'd)
General, Sir, I want to fight.

Houston, hat low against the light, clicks his heels and his horse starts down the street. Mathew struggles to keep up.

MATHEW (cont'd)
It's important. Tell me what I should do, Sir.

Houston finally looks down at him—

HOUSTON
You have a mother?

MATHEW
Yes, I do.

HOUSTON
And a father? You have one of those?

MATHEW
Yes, sir.

HOUSTON
Well, go home and be with them.

Houston spurs his horse on, leaving Mathew in the road. Toward the end of town he passes—

TWENTY MEN, mounted on their horses, JIM BOWIE, among them. The two men stare at each other for a long second—heading different directions. Then Bowie nods to Houston, spurs his horse and off gallop the twenty men.

Houston continues walking his horse out of town—one man headed away from the fray, the other toward it.

EXT. A HOUSE OUTSIDE OF TOWN—DAY

Travis's men—THIRTY or so—wait while Travis stands on the porch steps. A gen-tle couple—the AYERS—stand in the doorway. Charlie, with a little cloth suit-case in his hand, stares at Travis.

Travis leans down to his son's level. Straightens the lapels on the little boy's coat.

TRAVIS
Now you mind Mr. and Mrs. Ayers. Don't go causing any fuss.
(the boy slowly nods)
When I return we'll get a home of our own. I promise.
(quiet but intense)
One crowded hour of glorious life is worth an age without a name.

The boy nods again, hopeful. Nothing more to say. Travis, aware that his men are watching, holds out his hand.

TRAVIS (cont'd)
Good-bye, son.

Charlie shakes his father's hand. Travis stands to return to his horse.

CHARLIE
Daddy?...

TRAVIS
(stops, turns)
What, Charlie?

CHARLIE
(after a beat)
I just wanted to say it.

Travis, taken aback, can only nod. He get on his horse, motions for the men to ride.

With Travis—as he rides away, he never looks back. If he weren't surrounded by men he'd cry.

INT. COMMAND TENT—DAY

AN ORNATE OPIUM BOX is opened by General Antonio López de SANTA ANNA, vain, energetic, excessive even in patriotism. The general's secretary, RAMON CARO, pad in hand, hangs on his every word. Another general, MANUEL FERNANDEZ CASTRILLÓN, enters the tent.

> CASTRILLÓN (Spanish)
> General, we captured another group of rebels.

> SANTA ANNA (Spanish)
> Did you know this very box belonged to Napoleon Bonaparte?

The "tent" is luxurious, with fine furniture and china, silver cream pots, and chandeliers. On a shelf sits an ornate bust of Napoleon.

> CASTRILLÓN (Spanish)
> Yes, General.

Santa Anna allows himself a pinch. His eyes close and he sighs deeply.

> CASTRILLÓN (cont'd)
> (Spanish)
> Excellency, the citizens here are without food.

> SANTA ANNA (Spanish)
> They have rebelled against Mexico City, against me.

> CASTRILLÓN (Spanish)
> One might contend that an act of unexpected kindness might serve to secure their loyalty.

Castrillón is on shaky ground here (and he knows it). Santa Anna stares at Castrillón, then...

> SANTA ANNA (Spanish)
> Do they have shoes?

Castrillón looks to Caro, unsure where this is going.

> CASTRILLÓN (Spanish)
> Some do.

Santa Anna stands, looks to Caro.

> SANTA ANNA (Spanish)
> Santa Anna declares every man, woman, and child in this city will receive a new pair of sandals.

Caro transcribes the egalitarian gem as Santa Anna walks out.

EXT. COMMAND TENT—DAY

Santa Anna, followed by Castrillón and Caro, exits the tent. A colonel, JUAN ALMONTE, approaches, followed by a MESSENGER.

> ALMONTE (Spanish)
> Sir, there is a messenger from your brother-in-law, General Cos, Sir—

> SANTA ANNA (Spanish)
> (waving them off)
> Not now, Colonel.

Below him Mexican SOLDIERS viciously beat a PRISONER, dragging him back into a line of ZACATECAN REBELS standing before a waiting firing squad.

> SANTA ANNA (Spanish) (cont'd)
> Grace visits even the graceless, when they are about to die. I can feel its presence.

Ramon Caro writes it down.

> CASTRILLÓN (Spanish)
> Shall we have them draw lots, your excellency?

> SANTA ANNA (Spanish)
> Why?

> CASTRILLÓN (Spanish)
> To determine which shall be executed.

Santa Anna considers for a second, then...

> SANTA ANNA (Spanish)
> Execute them all.

Castrillón is visibly upset. Almonte passes the order along.

> CASTRILLÓN (Spanish)
> General, it is tradition that—

> SANTA ANNA (Spanish)
> If we follow tradition, the people in this place will remember that it was Fate that took their loved ones.

There is a VOLLEY of musket fire, followed by WAILING.

> SANTA ANNA (Spanish) (cont'd)
> Instead they will remember that it was Antonio López de Santa Anna.

> ALMONTE (Spanish)
> Sir, the messenger from General Cos?

Santa Anna nods. The Messenger steps forward...

> MESSENGER (Spanish)
> General of Brigade Cos has surrendered the Alamo and retreated from San Antonio de Bexar.

> SANTA ANNA (Spanish)
> Coward. If he were not family, I would slit his throat. Where is he now?

> MESSENGER (Spanish)
> Heading south. Toward us.

> SANTA ANNA (Spanish)
> (to Castrillón)
> Prepare the troops to march north.
> (after a beat)
> If the land pirates want blood, they will drown in it.

He turns to go to his tent. A thought...

> SANTA ANNA (Spanish)
> (cont'd)
> (points to bodies of rebels)
> See that no one touches those bodies for a week.

EXT. BEXAR PLAZA—DAY

Our first real look at the town and its beautiful plaza, now somewhat scarred from battle.

EXT. SOLEDAD STREET—DAY

Bowie and his men, including Seguin, ride down the street, amidst returning Tejano families. TEJANO CHILDREN see him, call out and run to touch his horse. Bowie eyes something ahead—the Veramendi house. SERGEANT WILLIAM WARD, tough, Bowie's right hand man, notices Bowie's gaze.

The men stop to dismount, but Bowie keeps riding toward the bullet-scarred home. The men notice...

> WARD
> Colonel?...Jimmy?...

> SEGUIN
> Leave him be.

INT. VERAMENDI HOUSE—DAY

Bowie dismounts, pushes open the door, observes holes in the roof and walls, empty liquor bottles, torn paper cartridges scattered everywhere. He walks through the main room and stands in the arch leading to the rear courtyard.

EXT. COURTYARD—DAY

Bowie walks into the middle of the courtyard—dead arbor, dirt, whiskey bottles. Bowie takes it in, lost in memories.

EXT. COURTYARD—FLASHBACK—NIGHT

Paper lanterns hang from the arbor, the three-man orchestra plays, Tejano wedding guests chat as Sam serves drinks. Bowie wears his wedding coat, chatting with Juan Seguin and his father-in-law, JUAN MARTIN de VERAMENDI. He turns to see—

URSULA, a beautiful 18-year-old Bexarena, steps onto the patio in her wedding dress, her sister JUANA by her side. The guests applaud but Ursula only has eyes for her husband.

We HOLD TIGHT ON Bowie's face as he watches her. The sky begins to lighten.

EXT. COURTYARD—WIDER—DAY (PRESENT)

It is day, and Bowie stands alone in the courtyard, the ruined arbor behind him. He looks out across his courtyard to the Alamo in the distance. Sam appears in the doorway.

SAM
You all right, Mr. James?—

BOWIE
(to himself)
I have a home.

SAM
Sir?

BOWIE
(again to himself)
I'm sorry, Sam. I can't blow the place up.

EXT. SAN ANTONIO DE BEXAR—DAY

Travis, riding at the head of twenty CAVALRY, enters town. They pass SHOPKEEPERS sweeping, PEOPLE rebuilding. Joe rides at the rear, every bit a horseman as the white soldiers.

A MUTT DOG (from the prologue) crosses the street to a man, TOM WATERS, who opens his coat and sneaks him scraps. Three drunk, dissipated NEW ORLEANS GREYS trade a bottle and laugh as Travis rides by. Travis brings his horse to a stop.

TRAVIS
Have the Quartermaster secure billeting.

The men start to dismount. Travis rides ahead.

FORSYTH
Where are you going, Sir?

TRAVIS
I'd like to see what I'm fighting for.

The men, unsure what he's talking about, dismount.

EXT. PORTRERO STREET—DAY

Travis arrives at the east end of town and stops his horse, staring straight ahead at something. We can tell from his look that it's important. He's staring at—

THE ALAMO in the distance. Battle-scarred but standing.

EXT. CHEROKEE TERRITORY—DAY

CHEERING. A wooden fish suspended in mid-air. A wooden ball SLAMS off of it. More CHEERING.

Two INDIANS with lacrosse-like sticks lunge for the wooden ball when it hits the grass.

The Cherokee TRIBE watches. It's a village of log cabins roofed with bark set along a river in a pine forest. Smoke puffs from the cabins.

A LONE HORSEMAN rides down the trail along the river. Houston nips at a bottle then puts it away. CHILDREN see the horseman and begin running toward him.

The "lacrosse" game halts, too. The men all stare at Houston as he rides into camp.

A CHEROKEE WOMAN nudges another woman, TALIHINA ROGERS, 30s, pretty, independent, who glances up at the rider—

WOMAN (Cherokee)
The Raven is back.

Talihina watches him stop his horse and stare at her. A history between these two.

INT. CABIN—DAY

A cozy cabin with hemp carpets, a table and stools made of poplar, and a broad bed covered with animal skins.

Houston sits on the bed, shirtless as Talihina gently removes his pants and sees a nasty, festering wound. Houston seems uncomfortable with her ministrations.

TALIHINA (Cherokee)
This has become much worse.

Houston can't even look down at the wound.

TALIHINA (Cherokee)
(cont'd)
Didn't your white wife ever dress it for you?

No need to respond: The answer is obvious. Talihina dips the cloth in a bowl of water, kneels and cleans the gaping wound.

EXT. ALAMO—OUTSIDE THE MAIN GATE—DAY

WE CRANE UP TO FIND Travis and J.C. NEILL, standing on the roof above the main gate. Neill points as he explains to Travis.

NEILL
It was founded as a mission a hundred years ago. The Bexarenos call it the Alamo after Alamo de Parras—a Spanish cavalry that moved in thirty years ago. As you can see, it was not designed with military intentions.

TRAVIS
It's well-armed.

NEILL
Most cannon of any fort west of the Mississippi.
(back to business)
General Cos left most of them. I've placed our largest, the 18-pounder, on the southwest wall, so it fronts the town. The north wall is in ruins, so I have two batteries with five cannon to defend it.
(points to east side)
What was the original Convento is now barracks and a makeshift infirmary. Let's walk, shall we?

EXT. ALAMO—COURTYARD—DAY (CONTINUOUS)

Neill and Travis walk across the courtyard, heading toward the mission. Nearby GREEN JAMISON, cleans his glasses while TWO MEN finish a fence made of wooden posts.

NEILL
Major Jamison, our Engineer, is emplacing a palisade between the main gate and the church.

TRAVIS
What was there before?

NEILL
Nothing. An indefensible flank.

TRAVIS
It still appears indefensible.

NEILL
Good riflemen and a 12-pounder should hold it.

A New Orleans Grey passes by in ragged uniform.

TRAVIS
Colonel, you should know that I have a uniform on order.
(off Neill's look)
One is as one appears.

Neill doesn't know what to make of this—as he himself isn't adorned in military garb. As they approach the old chapel...

NEILL
Church itself wasn't built until 1756.

TRAVIS
Was it destroyed in battle?
(off Neill's look)
It has no roof.

NEILL
The Catholics never quite finished it.

Neill nods to the statues on either side of the entrance.

NEILL (cont'd)
Saints Dominic and Francis. The locals tell me St. Francis had two gifts—prophecy and the ability to inspire passionate devotion.

Neill walks inside. Travis hesitates—takes a hard look at St. Francis—knowing he'll need both gifts.

INT. CHAPEL—DAY

Roofless with four rooms and a cannon ramp rising to the top of the back wall. Neill and Travis enter, walk...

NEILL
(points)
Baptistry, Sacristy.

They make their way up the ramp, look east over the wall.

NEILL (cont'd)
It is my conviction that holding this fort is the key to defending our colonies. As goes the Alamo, so goes Texas.

Travis nods, not sure he agrees.

NEILL ((cont'd)
If the need arises, I recommend you take my personal quarters on the west wall. They're isolated, yet close to the primary defenses.

TRAVIS
I'm afraid I don't understand, Sir.

NEILL
I have personal matters to attend to in Mina. I'm leaving you in command.

Travis takes this in—big news. He straightens up a bit.

NEILL (cont'd)
I know you fought this posting, Travis. Forting up's not exactly a cavalryman's dream.

TRAVIS
(committed)
I'll defend it with my life, Sir.

NEILL
(with a smile)
Your biggest task will be keeping volunteers and regulars from killing one another out of boredom.
(off Travis's look)
The Mexican army would have to cover 300 miles in the dead of winter to get here before I return.

A RAGGED FOOT TRUDGING THROUGH SNOW. AND THEN ANOTHER—

EXT. MEXICAN SCRUBLANDS—DAY

WE CRANE UP TO REVEAL Santa Anna's army on the march north. Proving Neill dead wrong.

INT. COUNCIL HOUSE—DAY

CHIEF BOWLES sits across from Houston. Soft couches are arranged in rows in a circle, the seats filled with WARRIORS. TWO BLACK SLAVES serve them as they talk.

CHIEF BOWLES
(Cherokee)
The Mexicans have treated us well. They respect our borders. They do not try to move us to ever worse lands. The Mexican government does not consider it legal to shoot Cherokee.

Houston gathers himself. He may be drunk. We see the faces of the warriors listening as he makes his pitch.

HOUSTON (Cherokee)
My friends, I realize this is not easy, to make a treaty with a country that isn't yet a country, with a nation that has no real government. But that is what I have come to ask.

Chief Bowles takes his time before answering.

CHIEF BOWLES
(Cherokee)
Raven, we fought together in the war against the Creek. I performed the ceremony when you took your Cherokee wife. We have even been to see the Great Father in Washington together.

HOUSTON (Cherokee)
We got to bill all that whiskey to the U.S. Government.

CHIEF BOWLES
(Cherokee)
There will be fighting in Texas, but it's not your fight. You were Cherokee long before you were Texian. The Cherokee are already a nation. Stay with us and be a representative for our people.

Bowles has made a convincing argument. Houston's POV, through the door, of the peaceful village outside.

EXT. CANTINA—ESTABLISHING—NIGHT

Travis looks at the cantina for a second, eyeing Bowie inside, then takes a deep breath and walks toward it.

INT. CANTINA—NIGHT

Local VAQUEROS and TEXIANS drink whiskey from glasses. GRIMES, with a neck actually red from the sun, tries to sell a long-rifle to a world-weary LOCAL.

GRIMES
This long tom will knock the whiskers off a hare at 200 yards. Mwee bwayno escopayta.

LOCAL (Spanish)
I'll need shot to go with it.

Grimes doesn't understand. JAMES BONHAM, dashing, steps in—

BONHAM
He wants you to throw in some shot.

GRIMES
Well then, you tell him them bottles of mescal better be full.

They make the transaction as Sam carries a fresh bottle of whiskey past. FOLLOW Sam toward a table in the corner where a grinning Bowie entertains a table full of his boys.

BOWIE
I'm right over there, one guy grabbing my neck while the other one's taking off half my ear with his one good tooth. The two I knocked out are gettin' up, realizing who knocked 'em out, so I look over my shoulder where I know my loyal man Ward is sure to be. What do I see—the tortilla lady and a 13-year-old hound dog.
(to Ward)
Where the hell were you?

WARD
I hate to tell you this, Jim, but you were in the wrong.

BOWIE
Which is exactly when I need you the most.

Laughter all around. Bowie grabs a pitcher from a passing waitress.

BOWIE (cont'd)
I love this place.

WARD
I love it, too, but at some point Texas is gonna be a state, but will it lean to the north or the south? We gonna have darkies working our fields or ain't we?

Sam pours another round, listening.

BOWIE
I've traded my share of flesh and I can promise you there will never be a free state that borders Louisiana.

Ward drinks to that. Bowie drinks, coughs, looks up, sees Travis entering, eyeing the rowdy volunteers. He spots Bowie, walks over, Joe in tow. When they arrive...

TRAVIS
Colonel...

JOE
(sotto; to Joe; proudly)
I stays in the room with Mr. Travis.

SAM
That quite a prize you got there.

TRAVIS
You look terrible.

Travis observes the somewhat decrepit Bowie.

TRAVIS (CONT'D)
Almost yellow. Right around the cheeks, forehead.

BOWIE
You doctoring, now? Along with everything else?

TRAVIS
I've heard rumor that you plan to destroy the mission and remove the cannon.

BOWIE
Oh, and where'd you hear that?

TRAVIS
Men tend to prattle on when they drink. Your men tend to drink.
(off Bowie's look)
It would be a great mistake.

BOWIE
I agree.
(off Travis's surprise)
And any further discussion on the matter will be between myself and Colonel Neill.

TRAVIS
Colonel Neill left Bexar this morning on personal business. It's my command now.

BOWIE
My, my, this is a swift rise, Billy.
(downs a shot)
Might wanna break out the long britches.

Ward shares a laugh with others. Joe turns away to save Travis embarrassment. Travis is stung, but recovers...

TRAVIS
Your men exhibit no discipline. If matters don't change it will become my duty, as colonel of this post to—

BOWIE
(correcting)
Lt. Colonel.

TRAVIS
Restrain your men. Or I will.

Travis walks away, followed by Joe. He passes Juan Seguin as he enters and walks up to Bowie's table.

SEGUIN
Santiago, sentries report seeing horses outside of town, in the Campo Santo.

Bowie downs his drink and rises.

EXT. OUTSIDE OF TOWN—NIGHT

Bowie and three ANGLOS, Seguin and three TEJANOS ride out into the darkness.

EXT. GRAVEYARD—NIGHT

Ancient headstones in very high grass. The SOUNDS of town fade as the men tether their horses in a copse of trees.

They draw their weapons and move stealthily forward until they hear HORSES and men WHISPERING.

BOWIE (Spanish)
(straining to hear)
Are they speaking Spanish?

SEGUIN (Spanish)
I can't make it out.

Movement behind a gravestone right in front of them. All WEAPONS point—

BOWIE (Spanish)
Don't move!

Suddenly, they hear weapons COCKED right behind them. Bowie turns, stares into fifteen long rifles. His men lower their weapons slowly to the ground. From behind a gravestone

CROCKETT
What's a feller have to do to...
(shouts)
Hablo Engles, muchachos?

MICAJAH AUTRY
We've got 'em, David.

From behind the gravestone steps DAVID CROCKETT, 49. Crockett and Bowie stare at each other in the murky light.

CROCKETT
Ease up on them weapons, boys. Appears we're all on the same side here.

BOWIE
What are you doing out here?

CROCKETT
Layin' low till we figgered out if it was Texians or Mexicans raising all the ruckus in town.
(beat)
David Crockett—

BOWIE
Crockett of Tennessee? Davy
Crockett?

Micajah Autry, great shot, refined, turns
to Bowie.

AUTRY
He prefers David.

EXT. BEXAR PLAZA—NIGHT

Bowie, Crockett, and their men are surrounded by people pouring out in the
street to see Davy Crockett.

CROCKETT
There was this little detail of a
reelection back home. You know
what I told them folks? I said,
you can all go to hell, I'm going
to Texas!

SCURLOCK
Hear that Colonel Bowie? Davy
Crockett's thrown in with Texas.

Crockett turns to Autry.

CROCKETT
(sotto; impressed)
Jim Bowie?...

Grimes appears with a copy of A Narrative of the Life of David Crockett and a
pen—

GRIMES
Put your mark in it, Mr. Crockett?

Crockett takes the book, signs—

SCURLOCK
I'm half alligator, half snapping
turtle. I can slide off a rainbow
and jump the Mississippi in a single leap. Davy... Tell 'em. How
you can whip your weight in wildcats. I seen you on the stage—

CROCKETT
That wasn't me.

SCURLOCK
Why, sure it was.

CROCKETT
That was an actor in a play, per-
forming a character—

SCURLOCK
Say the lines, Davy. "The Lion of
the West!"

Crockett eyes them with uncertainty.

GRIMES
I dare San-tanna to show his face
now that you're here!

CROCKETT
I had understood the fighting was
over.

(off their looks; hopeful)
Ain't it?...

EXT. SOUTH TEXAS—FIELD—DAY

On the horizon, TWO MEXICAN DRA-
GOONS on horseback approach a field
where a MEXICAN GRANDFATHER
plows with a team of oxen. The Dragoons arrive, stop, eye the old man.

HEAD DRAGOON (Spanish)
Hello, patriot. We were told you
have a son.

GRANDFATHER (Spanish)
My son was hanged. I am alone.

The Head Dragoon notices the lead to
the team of oxen lies on the ground. He
nods to the other Dragoon, who rides
over near a creek, looking around. The
Head Dragoon walks his horse slowly
around the old man, eyeing him.

GRANDFATHER (Spanish)
(cont'd)
I live in Tejas, but I am a loyal
Mexican.

The searching Dragoon WHISTLES. The
Head Dragoon rides over and looks
down into a ditch where a 15-year-old
boy, JESUS, hides.

HEAD DRAGOON (Spanish)
Welcome to the army of General
Antonio López de Santa Anna.

EXT. SOUTH TEXAS—DAY

The Mexican army again trudges north.
We see the foot soldiers, ragged, tired,
and among them—Jesus, now outfitted in
an ill-fitting uniform. Still scared. He
trades looks with others in the same boat:

A Yucatecan battalion—used to tropical
weather, now barefoot in the dead of
winter.

Other conscripts, some trudging forward
in chains.

AT THE HEAD OF THE MOVEMENT

Santa Anna raises a hand, stops, sits atop
his horse, alongside General Castrillón.
They watch as—

TWO RIDERS APPROACH. Behind the
riders, in the distance is General Cos's
retreating army.

GENERAL COS, tired, stops his horse facing Santa Anna.

SANTA ANNA (Spanish)
My wife asks me to give her use-
less brother a job and what hap-
pens? I end up in this shit-hole
Texas, again.

GENERAL COS (Spanish)
We were without supplies, your
Excellency. And the men were
dispirited—

SANTA ANNA (Spanish)
Turn your horse around, General.

GENERAL COS (Spanish)
I swore I would leave Tejas and
never return. I gave my—

SANTA ANNA (Spanish)
Turn it around!

Cos, beaten down, slowly turns the horse
and walks ahead. Santa Anna nods, a
trumpet blows and the army moves
north. The sounds of the Mexican band
becomes—

INT./EXT. CANTINA—BEXAR PLAZA—NIGHT

A band plays. A fandango is in progress.
Texians and Tejanos whirl brightly
dressed Tejana women under festive
lanterns.

SUSANNA DICKINSON, pretty, 19, and
her husband ALMERON, 40, dance, very
much in love. Almeron sees Crockett
work the crowd, shaking hands and
enduring many slaps on the back.

DICKINSON
Some of the men were speculat-
ing that he wants to be governor,
but I believe we'll be declaring
for a Republic, in which case
we'll need a President.

SUSANNA
He seems quite... common.

DICKINSON
Perhaps that's how he wants to
seem.

NEARBY

Seguin and Palaez stand in the corner
watching the festivities. Now that we
look at it through their eyes—their town
has been invaded by a very rough,
uncouth bunch.

PALAEZ (Spanish)
Why are you fighting for these
scum?

106

SEGUIN (Spanish)
My enemy's enemy is my friend. Santa Anna has betrayed the fatherland and murdered thousands, all Mexicans.

PALAEZ (Spanish)
But Santa Anna only wants to rule Mexico. These... these want the world.

Travis *passes the two* and moves through the crowd like a man who doesn't belong. He finds himself a spot to take in the festivities. A TEJANA PROSTITUTE eyes him.

Ward sees Travis, turns to Bonham...

WARD
Don't truck much with that feller.

BONHAM
I grew up with him.

(off Ward's look)
At least until his family moved to Alabama. I hadn't since laid eyes on him until we arrived here.

WARD
What was he like?

BONHAM
I think of Billy Travis I think of John Duncan's birthday party.

(off Ward's look)
The Duncan's threw a seventh birthday party for John—big affair—games, tents, a little circus—all set up in a field behind their house. Only children from the finest families were invited.

WARD
But not our Colonel Billy.

BONHAM
Day of the party, I look over to the edge of the field, off by himself, there's Billy, ragged clothes, no shoes, just standing—kinda like he is now. Party lasted all day, when it was over, sun going down, I was leaving with my parents, looked back over my shoulder.

(after a beat)
Hadn't moved so much as an inch in five hours. Stubborn.

WARD
What in the hell was that about?

BONHAM
Don't know—maybe he just wanted to tell everybody he'd been to John Duncan's birthday party. But I'd venture a guess if you asked him today he'd remember a helluva lot more about it than I do.

TRAVIS Spies Crockett, seeks a moment with the "popular kid."

TRAVIS
Congressman Crockett, you should know that I intend to complete the necessary paperwork to make you a colonel in our volunteer forces.

CROCKETT
Seems to me we got more'nough colonels. High private suits me just fine.

The band finishes and one of the PLAYERS motions to Crockett.

TRAVIS
I respect that, but with your reputation—

Crockett holds up a finger to the band leader—

CROCKETT
(already on the move)
Let's you and me have a good long chat about this later, all right, Travers?

Travis doesn't correct the mispronunciation, just watches as Crockett walks away; steps on the box to cheers.

CROCKETT (cont'd)
Ladies and gentlemen—this is my first time at one of these Texian fandangos—and I promise to keep this speech shorter than an Irishman's temperance vow!

(laughter)
Me and my mounted volunteers sure do 'preciate the warm hospitality we been shown since we got here—and if this Santanner and his bunch should drop by, we'll make it right warm for them, too!

(cheers and applause)
We will lick them like fine salt!

(more cheers)
Now contrary to popular opinion, I'm not that much as a fighter—

Cries of "No! Not true!" Crockett watches and smiles. Bowie watches with a more straight face.

CROCKETT (cont'd)
And we all know I wasn't cut out for politics, being the only congressman that ever left Washington poorer than what he come. Fortunately, I ran into my good friend, Sam Houston, who said, Davy—David—get on down there to Texas and show them folks how "The Tennessee Grasshopper" is really played—

He raises a fiddle and begins to expertly saw away at an infectious, upbeat mountain tune.

People begin dancing, except for Jim Bowie who turns to the man next to him.

BOWIE
Bear hunter wanders into town, you'd think it's the second coming.

Ward walks up to Bowie, whispers in his ear. Bowie's face shows disbelief, then anger. He forges through the crowd grabs Travis shoulder, spins him around—face to face.

BOWIE (cont'd)
You don't have the sand to *talk* to two of my men, much less arrest them.

TRAVIS
I told you I intended to restore order.

BOWIE
You have no command over my volunteers!

TRAVIS
I have absolute command!

Travis walks out of the cantina.

BOWIE
(to his men)
Break 'em out!

This stops Travis cold. Bowie steps into the door. A crowd has gathered, surrounding the two. Crockett notices the commotion, jumps down from the box. The music stops.

BOWIE (cont'd)
It'll be a cold day in hell when I take orders from a debtor who leaves a pregnant wife in the dead of night!

TRAVIS
Or I from a land swindler who marries a girl—rest her soul—for her family's money!

That's it—Bowie tosses off his coat, takes out his knife and sticks into in a table. Crockett jumps in.

> **CROCKETT**
> Whoa, fellas! Just cause we got nobody to fight, don't mean we start looking to our right and left.

Bowie stares, not backing down. Travis sizes up the situation.

> **TRAVIS**
> Congressman Crockett has a point. We should do this demo-cratically. A vote.

Bowie relaxes a bit, almost smiles.

> **SCURLOCK**
> Crockett! We want Crockett!

Bowie's smiles drops.

> **CROCKETT**
> Naw, naw, I'm *with* you boys, not over you.

> **BOWIE**
> All for the *Lieutenant* Colonel, raise your hands!

Travis tries to read the situation, looks around. After a few seconds.

> **TRAVIS**
> Come on, men. No repercussions. All in favor of me commanding?...

Slowly a few hands raise, but not many. In the corner, Joe looks left, right, hoping for more hands.

> **BOWIE**
> All for me?!

A majority of hands, including most of Travis's men. Travis, humiliated, looks to Crockett, who holds up two palms.

> **CROCKETT**
> The gentleman from Tennessee respectfully abstains.

Bowie grins. The crowd reacts, slapping backs as Bowie puts his jacket back on. But Travis can't take it—

> **TRAVIS**
> You can command the militia only. The regulars can't be led by a volunteer. It's illegal.

Travis knows how lame this sounds. Men SCOFF.

> **BOWIE**
> Don't like the outcome, you change the rules. Is that it, Buck?

> **WARD**
> Don't fret about it, Jim. We all know who's in charge.

Bowie considers, then as his first official order—

> **BOWIE**
> (to Travis)
> Release my men!

Travis slowly nods to FORSYTH, one of his men. Then, tail between his legs, he walks through the crowd and into the night. WE SEE, in the shadows, the TEJANO PROSTITUTE from the party. Travis sees her, too, stops, trades a look with her.

EXT. BEXAR STREET—LATER—NIGHT

Now quiet. Crockett and his Ten-nesseans, a little worse for wear, weave down the street on foot.

> **CROCKETT**
> I'll put in for that parcel on the Red River—the one we passed on the way to here. The one with that blue hole at the elbow.

The men nod and grunt agreement.

> **MICAJAH AUTRY**
> Don't know why we had to tent up outside of town when there's so many fine houses with big cornhusk beds just sitting empty.

> **CROCKETT**
> Why they empty?

> **MICAJAH AUTRY**
> Folks hereabout believe the Mexi-cans are comin' back. But most of the boys think they won't be here 'til late spring, if they come at all.

As they pass a small house—door and windows open. Inside—

Ana and GREGORIO ESPARZA bury sil-ver in a hole in the dirt floor. Crockett watches with some trepidation.

> **CROCKETT**
> Figger they know something we don't?

INT. TRAVIS'S BEDROOM—NIGHT

The room is dark (save one candle). Travis, without a shirt, sits on the edge of his bed, staring into the dark, the Tejano prostitute sleeping behind him.

Travis stares straight ahead, then his face starts to change from defeated to deter-mined. He licks his thumb and puts out the candle. As it sputters, leaving the room dark...

EXT. ON A HILL—NIGHT

A Mexican DRAGOON (Head Dragoon) crests a hill, stops, smiles at what he sees... In the distance—the lights of Bexar.

EXT. BEXAR—DAWN

The town is QUIET. Suddenly, in the San Fernando Church Tower, the bell RINGS and RINGS and RINGS.

EXT. BEXAR—DAWN

Soldiers and townspeople come slowly into the streets, all staring toward the bell-tower of the San Fernando Church. Travis sprints across the plaza to the church.

INT./EXT. BELLTOWER STAIRS—CUPOLA

Travis reaches the top. The RINGING slowly dies out. A SENTRY, DANIEL CLOUD, stares into the distance, confused.

> **DANIEL CLOUD**
> I saw glints of metal. That way. I know I did. Then I looked again and didn't see nothin'.

Travis leaves the cupola, walks across the church roof to the west end. He stops, looks—

In the far distance—maybe two, maybe five miles away—the Mexican army crest-ing a hill. Like an army of ants.

Bowie races up, coughing. He stands beside Travis, looks out—sees the same thing as Travis. Bowie grows stoic.

> **BOWIE**
> On the plus side of the ledger, Buck, I just found the miracle cure for a hangover.

> **TRAVIS**
> (after a beat)
> We'll never be able to defend the town.

EXT. PLAZA (BEXAR)—DAY

Bedlam. Soldiers, civilians in disarray. Travis rides through, trying for calm, try-ing to get people to listen.

> **TRAVIS**
> Orderly withdrawal. Orderly withdrawal to the Alamo! We will proceed in an orderly with-drawal.

Nobody listens to Travis. Joe keeps up on foot. Shouts and people running out of the way—we PAN to see a small herd of longhorns being driven through the plaza. Crockett's men herd the cattle. Crockett, on foot, keeps things moving.

> **CROCKETT**
> Keep them beeves out of the buildin's! Go, go, keep 'em movin'!

He nods to a TEJANO WOMAN cowering against the wall.

> **CROCKETT** *(cont'd)*
> We be out of your path directly, ma'am. Mind them horns.

He passes Grimes who wrestles his rifle back from the local.

> **GRIMES**
> I know I sold it, but now I need it back.

We are SWEPT ACROSS the plaza with Almeron and Susanna, infant Angelina in her arms. Joe jumps in to help her hand the baby to Almeron, on horseback, then jump up herself.

Travis, stunned by the chaos, reaches for order.

> **TRAVIS**
> Orderly withdrawal...

Tom Waters passes Travis chasing the mutt dog.

> **WATERS**
> Come here, Salvador. Come here.

Seguin and his men unload corn from a warehouse into wagons.

> **TRAVIS**
> Captain Seguin. Get your men into the Alamo!

> **SEGUIN**
> You can starve by yourself, Colonel, but I'm bringing the corn.

Travis rides on, passing a TEJANO WOMAN holding the hand of a CHILD as they watch Anglos stream to the Alamo.

> **CHILD** (Spanish)
> Are they going to die, Mama?

> **TEJANO WOMAN** (Spanish)
> Every one of them.

EXT. VERAMENDI HOUSE—DAY

Sam tosses food and utensils into a cart. SOUND OF RETCHING. Bowie is sick. He wipes his mouth with a cloth and JUANA, his sister-in-law, sees it's blood red.

Bowie ignores her and continues loading a small arsenal of firearms into a cart.

> **BOWIE** (Spanish)
> There's a shotgun hidden in the commune.

EXT. AT THE RIVER—DAY

Cattle are herded through the water.

EXT. POTRERO STREET—HIGH ANGLE—DAY

Travis joins the river of refugees heading toward the Alamo.

EXT. ALAMO—COURTYARD—DAY

Frantic activity as people, animals, and supplies pour through the main gate. Gregorio Esparza leads Ana and the family inside. She looks uneasily at the disorganized Texians, crosses herself.

INT. CHAPEL—BAPTISTRY—DAY (CONTINUOUS)

Dickinson leads his wife, baby, and several OTHER WOMEN inside to the baptistry.

> **DICKINSON**
> Thick walls. You'll be safe here.

He shares a look with his wife, kisses her and the baby.

EXT. ALAMO COURTYARD—DAY (CONTINUOUS)

There is confusion between regulars and volunteers.

> **FORSYTH**
> Get up there. Get over there. I don't care where you get, but get.

> **WARD**
> I answer to Bowie!
> (to himself)
> Wherever he is.

EXT. ALAMO—MAIN GATE—DAY

In the confusion, Jim Bowie, Green Jameson, and Seguin stand by the main gate while ANIMALS, PEOPLE stream by. Seguin writes on a page of paper while Bowie dictates.

> **BOWIE**
> "...under guarantee of a white flag which I believe will be respected by you and your forces."

Seguin writes in Spanish.

> **BOWIE** *(cont'd)*
> "God and Mexico—"

Bowie reconsiders, grabs the paper, lines through something.

> **BOWIE** *(cont'd)*
> Make that "God and Texas." Ah hell, when was there somebody I couldn't talk to?
> (to Jameson)
> Find something white.

INT. ALAMO—TRAVIS'S HEADQUARTERS—DAY

Travis sits at his desk writing a letter.

> **TRAVIS** (V.O.)
> The enemy in large force are in sight. We want men and provisions. Send them to us. We have 150 men and are determined to defend the Alamo to the last.

Ward and Grimes, OTHERS, hustle past Travis's office—

> **WARD**
> We're under attack and yore majesty locks hisself in his room.

We hold on Travis who seals the letter, grabs another sheet and begins to write. Joe paces in the background.

> **TRAVIS**
> Joe, sit down before that terror catches.

> **CROCKETT**
> Colonel?

Travis looks up, sees Crockett in the doorway—

> **CROCKETT** *(cont'd)*
> Don't mean to disturb, but we got a mare's nest out here.

> **TRAVIS**
> I have to get couriers out while there's still time.
> (off Crockett's look)
> You and your men will defend the palisade.

> **CROCKETT**
> That little old wood fence?

> **TRAVIS**
> You prefer a different assignment?

> **CROCKETT**
> Naw, that's the one I was gonna put in for.

TRAVIS

If you could oversee manning the walls it would be a help.

(off Crockett's nod)
We should have six men to a cannon. Eighteen tubes, which works out to—

CROCKETT

Hundred and eight men.

TRAVIS

And we should have a man with a musket every 4 feet of wall.

CROCKETT

(after a beat)
We're gonna need more men.

EXT. BEXAR—PLAZA—DAY

The Mexican Army—hundreds and hundreds—makes its way into the plaza in parade formation. Santa Anna rides front and center, alongside COLONEL JOSE BATRES, an aide.

SANTA ANNA (Spanish)

They scattered like frightened children.

Santa Anna eyes the locals peering from windows and doorways. The Tejano woman and child we saw before—

TEJANO WOMAN (Spanish)

(to the child)
Say it, say it, just like we practiced!

CHILD (Spanish)

Viva Santa Anna! Viva Mexico!

Santa Anna nods at the acclaim, feeling confidant. He spots a STUNNING YOUNG TEJANA, maybe 16, in a doorway. Santa Anna smiles. The girl's mother drags her inside and closes the door. Santa Anna looks to Batres, who nods, message received.

AT THE CHURCH

Castrillón and Almonte watch admiringly as Santa Anna rides.

CASTRILLÓN (Spanish)

What other man could have made this march? Every time I question him I am reminded of his greatness.

Santa Anna arrives and with help from an orderly, dismounts.

SANTA ANNA (Spanish)

Are the advance troops encamped?

(off Castrillón's nod)
Battery placement spotted?

CASTRILLÓN (Spanish)

Yes, your Excellency, but it may not be necessary.

(off Santa Anna's look)
It appears the Texians may desire a parley. We should respond with terms.

(off Santa Anna's disgust)
What are your terms, General?

EXT. OUTSIDE ALAMO—DAY

A WHITE FLAG bounces along—carried by Jameson and Bowie—riding toward town. They stop at the River Bridge and wait the approach of two Mexican riders.

EXT. RIVER BRIDGE—DAY

Castrillón and Almonte arrive at the bridge to meet Bowie and Jamison. Even before the Mexicans come to a stop—

BOWIE (Spanish)

(to Castrillón)
Manuel, how many times we gonna trade this old church back and forth before this war is over?

Castrillón can barely look at Bowie.

INT. TRAVIS'S QUARTERS—DAY

Travis hands letters to COLORADO SMITH and another TEXIAN.

TRAVIS

To Gonzales, and to Colonel Fannin at Goliad. Godspeed.

As they race away LIEUTENANT FORSYTH races to the door.

FORSYTH

Colonel, I think you should see this.

WE FOLLOW Travis from his quarters to the SW wall ramp, UP THE RAMP to the battery. AS WE SWIRL AROUND HIM WE SEE—

AS FAR AS THE EYE CAN SEE—THE MEXICAN ARMY. Putting up tents, erecting cannon placement—LANCERS and DRAGOONS move to and fro on horseback. We've never seen so many people.

Travis tries not to sweat as he looks upon a truly awesome and terrifying sight. Crockett, also in awe, slides in next to Travis.

CROCKETT

We're gonna need a LOT more men.

TRAVIS

(almost to himself)
Now that is a handsome Army.

ON THE BRIDGE

Bowie discusses business...

BOWIE (Spanish)

I've come out to see if your commander would be willing to parley out of this unfortunate situation.

Castrillón still avoiding. Almonte dismounts and hands Bowie a piece of paper.

ALMONTE (Spanish)

From General Santa Anna himself.

Bowie opens the note and starts to read.

ON THE SOUTHWEST BATTERY

Travis spots Bowie.

TRAVIS

What is Colonel Bowie doing on the bridge?

WARD

Trying to get us out of this mess.

TRAVIS

Fire the 18-pounder.

FORSYTH

Sir?

TRAVIS

You heard me. Fire the cannon.

Almeron Dickinson and his TEAM quickly prep the cannon. The primer sparks.

ON THE BRIDGE

Bowie finishes the letter—bad news—looks to Castrillón.

BOWIE

Manuel?...

CASTRILLÓN (Spanish)

I'm sorry, Santiago.

A CANNON BLASTS. All four men react.

INT. BEXAR PLAZA—DAY

Santa Anna barely flinches, watches as— THE CANNON BALL hits a small house east of town. Santa Anna turns to Batres.

SANTA ANNA (Spanish)

Raise the flag!

BATRES (Spanish)
Which one, General?

EXT. ON THE BRIDGE—DAY
All four men steady their horses.

BOWIE
Goddamn! Manuel...

(in Spanish)
I had nothing to do with that!

Castrillón and Almonte whirl their horses away and Bowie and Jameson do the same.

TWO HANDS SUPPORTING TWO ANKLES. We're—

EXT. BEXAR PLAZA—DAY
WE CRANE UP past the ankles, to legs, to an arm holding tight and then to another arm and above it—as it is attached—

A RED FLAG WITH SKULL AND CROSS-BONES blows in the wind. AS WE PULL BACK WE SEE the flag is on top of the San Fernando Church as, in the background, still more troops march in.

EXT. ALAMO MAIN GATE—DAY
Bowie races in on horseback, jumps down, races up the ramp to where Travis stands.

BOWIE
Are you a fool?! I was trying to get us a truce!

TRAVIS
(angry, loud)
If we broker a cessation, we'll do so from a position of strength, not weakness. We don't turn belly up and beg. Otherwise we have said nothing and this conflict means nothing!

As much as Travis loves to make a speech is how much Bowie hates rhetoric.

BOWIE
Dying for nothing means shit to me.

TRAVIS
(eyes the letter)
Their response?

Bowie sticks it out, Travis takes it, reads, looks up—

TRAVIS (cont'd)
...Surrender at discretion...

(beat; with half a smile)
Perhaps, Colonel, they'll only execute officers?

Dickinson notices, and then the men notice, the skull and crossbones flag flying above the belltower.

CROCKETT
Looks like we all just got promoted.

PAN DOWN THE WALL where the Tejanos are watching as well.

GREGORIO ESPARZA (Spanish)
I saw General Cos. He has broken his promise not to return.

SEGUIN (Spanish)
A man should keep his word.

(after a beat)
Is your brother with them?

GREGORIO ESPARZA (Spanish)
Maybe he raised the flag.

SOUTHWEST BATTERY
Travis, Crockett and Bowie still there with others. Bowie and Crockett look at each other, then in unison, to Travis, who feels their stare—"Well, now what?"

TRAVIS
We wait for reinforcements. Within a few days all of Texas will know our situation.

BOWIE
Tell me, Buck, in Alabama, precisely how many is "a few"?

Travis ignores the remark.

TRAVIS
Gentlemen, I suggest we man our posts and prepare for a response not made of cloth.

Travis walks away, leaving Bowie and Crockett to trade looks.

CROCKETT
You figger that fancy talk just comes off the top of his head?

BOWIE
I've never been too fond of the heroic gesture.

A MEXICAN CANNON fires—a puff of smoke from a Mexican position and then—

A ball clears the wall and BLASTS INTO the long barracks.

INT. CHURCH BAPTISTRY—DAY (CONTINUOUS)
Susannah Dickinson holds her crying baby, while she and other WOMEN

cower together—dust flying all around them.

EXT. YTURRI HOUSE—DAY
Mexican soldiers are carting Santa Anna's belongings into this house on the plaza. TWO MEN unload crates from a cart.

BATRES (Spanish)
Careful with the general's crystal! Broken bones for broken glass.

They start to handle the crates oh-so-carefully. WE FOLLOW a crate—

INSIDE YTURRI HOUSE
A WAR COUNCIL in progress. Santa Anna, Castrillón, Almonte, GENERAL SESMA, Cos and the ever-present Caro. They sit/stand around a table in the middle of the main room. Santa Anna's BLACK MANSERVANT serves them coffee.

SANTA ANNA (Spanish)
Is Houston with them?

ALMONTE (Spanish)
No.

Santa Anna takes this in, almost smiles, sips his coffee.

SANTA ANNA (Spanish)
I heard that his young wife deserted him. Because he has a wound that never heals.

ALMONTE (Spanish)
He left office rather than answer to the scandal.

SANTA ANNA (Spanish)
What kind of man gives up power for a woman? He will come. If only to salvage his reputation. What of Jim Bowie, the knife fighter?

ALMONTE (Spanish)
Inside the mission. And someone else of worth... Congressman Davy Crockett.

SANTA ANNA (Spanish)
Crockett? The great bear killer?!

(off Almonte's nod)
Excellent.

ALMONTE (Spanish)
They are disorganized and outmanned. We should take advantage immediately.

CASTRILLÓN (Spanish)
We have heavy cannon arriving in a few days. They aren't going anywhere.

ALMONTE (Spanish)
There are 400 more rebels less than a week's march from here, at Goliad, under Colonel Fannin.

SANTA ANNA (Spanish)
Houston, Fannin—more meat for the spit. We wait. But we will make the dark a nightmare to remind them of the truth yet to come.

EXT. ALAMO—VARIOUS SHOTS—DAY

• Travis walking the north wall batteries

• Crockett and the Tennesseans at the Palisade. They're watching the Mexican army move into positions. It all seems quite lackadaisical.

MICAJAH AUTRY
Just as soon take my chances fighting out there in the open.

CROCKETT
I don't like being hemmed in any more'n you. But here we sit.

Crockett notices Bowie sitting outside his room, his men huddled around him, receiving instructions.

BOWIE
Don't get clustered up—be aware of crossfire. Fill your loading blocks with grease-patched balls—we may be firing fast. Stack your muskets but don't powder them—ten minutes in this damp air and they'll be nothing but sticks.

He grabs a bottle of whiskey from one of the men, holds it out...

BOWIE (cont'd)
And no more of *this*. None. Now git.

The men go to their posts. Bowie takes a swig from the bottle. Sam urges the bottle from him as he sets a smoking kettle on the ground beneath Bowie. Bowie groans as Sam drapes a blanket over Bowie's head and urges him down so the smoke from the kettle fills his lungs. After a second or two he comes up coughing.

BOWIE (cont'd)
No more.

Bowie notices Crockett nearby, eyeing him.

CROCKETT
Hi'dy. Seems we have a friend in common.
(nothing from Bowie)
Sam... Houston.

BOWIE
(still nothing)
Seems so.

Bowie coughs up phlegm. Crockett approaches.

CROCKETT
What ails you, Jim, exactly?

BOWIE
Consumption, typhoid, pneumonia. One or all. Exactly.

Bowie sees that Crockett is eyeing his knife. Bowie pulls back his coat, slips it out without even looking. He offers it to Crockett, who examines it.

CROCKETT
That knife fight you was in, at that Sandbar in Natchez, the one that got written up.... Was all that true?

BOWIE
You don't believe everything you read, now do ya?

CROCKETT
I didn't read it. I heard it... And what I heard was that he put a sword cane and two shots in you.

BOWIE
I don't remember.

CROCKETT
Figger we'll see Sam soon enough. When he gets here we'll have us a good ol' time.

Bowie just stares in disbelief at Crockett. Then he leans forward.

BOWIE
It was three shots, a sword cane through the lung and one through the hand. And then I cut his heart out.
(Bowie eyes the ridge)
Those ain't bears out there. You understand that.... Don't you, David?

MICAJAH AUTRY
Why in the hell don't they just attack us?

BOWIE
I seen vacqueros spend all day killing one bull.

DISSOLVE TO:

THE SUN SETS SLOWLY. WE HEAR THE STRAINS OF DEGUELLO.

EXT. ALAMO—VARIOUS SHOTS

Around the wall—men listening to the music.

WARD
You bring a band you're counting on having something to celebrate.

EXT. ON A HILL—DUSK

Santa Anna's band plays the haunting tune.

EXT. SOUTHWEST BATTERY—DUSK/NIGHT

Crockett walks up, joins Travis, as they listen together.

CROCKETT
Mighty nice of them to serenade us like this.

TRAVIS
It's a cavalry march, but I'm told Santa Anna fancies it for other uses. He borrowed it from the Spaniards, the Spaniards from the Moors. It's called Deguello.

CROCKETT
Kinda purty.

TRAVIS
"Deguello" means "*Slit. Throat.*"

CROCKETT
It ain't *that* purty.

The music ends. There is an ominous silence all around the courtyard and then—A FULL-SCALE CANNON ATTACK

A CANNONBALL hits the north wall, kicking up rubble. Another, with a fuse BURNING, lands in the courtyard. There is a moment of anticipation—all eyes on the bomb. And then—

IT EXPLODES, sending shrapnel in all directions. Pieces of metal blast into walls, doorways.

EXT. VARIOUS MEXICAN CANNON PLACEMENTS—NIGHT (CONTINUOUS)

One, two, three cannons fire from different positions into and at the Alamo.

INTERCUT WITH:

EXT. ALAMO—VARIOUS WALLS—NIGHT (CONTINUOUS)

The north wall, the west wall, the Palisade—all hit with cannon fire. Dust, destruction. Waters grabs his mutt and dives for cover. INTERCUT WITH:

INT. ALAMO—VARIOUS ROOMS—NIGHT (CONTINUOUS)

Men, women, children cowering—at the walls, in the baptistry, in the long barracks.

INT. TRAVIS'S QUARTERS—NIGHT (CONTINUOUS)

Joe sits in a corner of the room, his hands over his ears, his face in a grimace.

EXT. MEXICAN CANNON PLACEMENT—NIGHT (CONTINUOUS)

Jesus, crying from the din of noise, throwing water on each cannon after it's fired. He slumps to the ground, crying, screaming. The screams become—

INT. ALAMO BAPTISTRY—DAWN

The SCREAMS of a baby. Little Angelina Dickinson nestles against her mother and quiets. And mysteriously...so do the explosions. The women all exchange glances—is it over?

EXT. ALAMO COURTYARD—DAY (CONTINUOUS)

The courtyard is empty, the silence is deafening. And then one by one, two by two, people emerge from their cubby holes into the light. It's over. For now.

At the Palisade, Crockett rises up to look out at the quiet. After a beat he turns, walks over to the palisade, steps up and peers over the fence.

The Mexican army—still there in numbers—campfires, tents, dragoons on horseback.

Crockett just stares at the enemy. Autry steps up beside him and takes a look himself.

CROCKETT
Morning.

AUTRY
Morning.

EXT. NORTH WALL—LATER—DAY

Green Jameson and others work to refortify the damaged wall with mud and sticks. On top of the wall, Ward and others cover them and look out at the Mexican troops.

WARD
Notice anything different about them cannon?
    (off his friend's look)
They moved 'em closer last night.

Sure enough the mound of dirt protecting the cannon placements has advanced.

A SPADE HITS HARD DIRT.

TRAVIS (V.O.)
That would be the spot.

EXT. COURTYARD—DAY

Travis walks past Sam and Joe, starting to dig a well.

TRAVIS
As our well is drying, any day you find yourself not busy with other matters, you need to be digging a new one here.

SAM
    (after he's gone)
Ain't bad enuf we got to fetch 'em the water, now we got to find it, too.
    (sees Joe digging)
Don't work so hard.

JOE
Sooner I get down this hole, sooner my head don't get taken off.

SAM
Sooner you get a bunch of white men they drinkin' water, sooner you get a pat on the head.
    (beat)
He had you long?

JOE
Mr. Simon White down at Brazoria hold my contrack an' he hire me out to Mr. William last July.

SAM
I knew a man name Nemo belong to Simon White run off for Saltillo.

JOE
Did he make it?

SAM
I wish I knew, but I don't.

INT. ALAMO COURTYARD—DAY (CONTINUOUS)

A Texian, at a forge, chops up horseshoes, chains, anything that can be used in a cannon. Daniel Cloud retrieves the shrapnel from a water bucket and puts handfuls of it in canvas bags. Travis walks by. . . .

TRAVIS
There are two leaden troughs in the horse pens. Should make fine cannon shot.

After he's gone...

DANIEL CLOUD
What in the hell are we saving our cannon balls for?

EXT. ANOTHER PART OF COURTYARD—DAY (CONTINUOUS)

Travis hears COUGHING. Follows the sound around to—

EXT. ALAMO—NEAR TRAVIS'S QUARTERS—DAY

Travis finds Bowie against a wall, coughing. He slaps the wall in disgust over his condition. Travis gives Bowie a minute to compose himself, then walks over.

Bowie looks up, wipes his mouth.

BOWIE
Notice how you don't really hear it until it stops?

TRAVIS
    (after a beat; honest)
I've never been in a cannon battle before. Not of this magnitude.

Bowie realizes this is an olive branch of sorts. But before he can respond with anything nice—

TRAVIS (cont'd)
Until they decide to attack, I suspect we'll be bombarded on a nightly basis. Deprive us of sleep.

BOWIE
'Til we start seeing ghosts everywhere.

TRAVIS
Colonel, I became a little heated with you in front of your men. It was ill-advised and not terribly professional.

BOWIE
Forget it. Most of 'em didn't understand what you were saying anyway.

TRAVIS

It's important that you and I agree. For me, though we are poorly supplied, surrender is not an option. I submit that we engage and delay until reinforcements arrive.

Bowie nods agreement. After a beat, Travis nods back, amazed that the two have reached consensus.

BOWIE

Sometimes it's just the *way* you say things, Travis. That's all, I swear to God.

Bowie walks away, leaving Travis to ponder the statement.

EXT. ALAMO—VARIOUS SHOTS—DUSK

Deguello begins. Faces, listening, knowing what will come next. And then...*It does*.

VARIOUS SHOTS—balls hitting walls.

VARIOUS SHOTS—Mexican positions firing cannons one after another. OFF THE BOOM OF A CANNON—

EXT. INDIAN CAMP—DAY

Two arrows lie on the ground. One arrowhead is barbed, the other is smooth. Sam Houston, squatting, drinking from a bottle, watches two Indian BOYS, six, look at the arrowheads.

INDIAN BOY (Cherokee)

This one is for birds?

HOUSTON (Cherokee)

That's right.

INDIAN BOY (Cherokee)

And this one is for fishing.

HOUSTON (Cherokee)

No.

INDIAN BOY (Cherokee)

Is it for very big birds?

HOUSTON (Cherokee)

It is for men.

Houston sees a circling bird, picks up the bird arrow and draws it back on a bow. From above we see the bird—A RAVEN.

Houston, bow drawn, stares at the bird for several seconds then slowly lowers it. He hears something, turns, sees DEAF SMITH—riding toward him. We stay with the boys as the two men greet one another, then we're with Houston...

DEAF SMITH

Santa Anna has captured Bexar.

HOUSTON

When?

DEAF SMITH

Three days ago. Our troops are forted up in the Alamo.

The news hits Houston hard.

EXT. INDIAN CAMP—OUTSIDE OF CAMP—DAY

Chief Bowles sits, staring at the river. Houston walks over.

HOUSTON (Cherokee)

How did I come by my Indian name?

BOWLES (Cherokee)

The Raven is proud and dark. And alone.

That was you as a boy, when you first came to us.

HOUSTON (English)

And now?

BOWLES (English)

Now they have another name for you... Ootstetee Ardeetahskee

HOUSTON (English)

(almost to himself)
The Big Drunk.

BOWLES (English)

In the stories, the Raven is often cursed—he is beaten and crushed and left for dead. But in the end he outwits his enemy.

Houston looks at Bowles. What is the old man getting at?

BOWLES (English)
(cont'd)

Of course that is only in stories. And you are the Raven no more.

Off Houston's look—

EXT. INDIAN CAMP—DAY

Houston, dressed again in his Anglo clothes, mounts his horse and turns to Talehina. They share a look.

TALEHINA (Cherokee)

Don't return here. Your pride has chosen for you.

Houston almost smiles then slowly walks the horse away. The walk turns into a lope, then a gallop as he disappears.

EXT. ALAMO—WEST WALL—DAY

Seguin, Esparza, and other men from his company look over the wall and talk to AN OLD WOMAN, standing below, outside the wall.

SEGUIN (Spanish)

They let you come and go as you please?

OLD WOMAN (Spanish)

I am too old to matter. Four months ago they were here and you were there.

(points behind her to Bexar)
Then they left here and you were still there. Now they are there and you are here. I'm too old to care anymore.

SCURLOCK

Ask her what in hell they're waiting for.

SEGUIN (Spanish)

Do you see any preparations for attack? What are they doing?

OLD WOMAN (Spanish)

The generals eat, the army starves.

Seguin looks to Scurlock, shrugs. SCURLOCK, antsy, has had enough—stands—

SCURLOCK

Come on! Fight! We're waiting! Yer yeller—every Mescan is yeller!

He realizes what he's said, turns sheepishly to Seguin's men.

SEGUIN

We're all Mexicans, Scurlock. Remember well the oath you took.

(to the old woman; Spanish)
Next time bring tortillas!

SCURLOCK

This is one crazy mess.

EXT. BEXAR PLAZA—DAY

Batres makes his way across the plaza, passing carts, chickens, locals. He adjusts his jacket, walks up to the door of a house and knocks.

The mother of the stunning Tejana opens it, her daughter peering from behind. Batres smiles.

BATRES (V.O.) (Spanish)
She is even more beautiful upon inspection.

EXT. PORTRERO STREET—DAY

Santa Anna rides with Batres toward the front lines.

BATRES (Spanish)
But her father is dead and her mother will not let her daughter see you. Unless…

SANTA ANNA (Spanish)
Unless?

BATRES (Spanish)
Unless you marry her first. Unfortunate.

SANTA ANNA (Spanish)
I think the ceremony should be simple. Do you agree?

BATRES (Spanish)
But, General, by your order we brought no priests with us…. And… you are already married… to General Cos's sister?

(off Santa Anna's hard look)
A simple ceremony, yes.

SANTA ANNA (Spanish)
The men will be happy to see me.

EXT. PALISADE—DAY

Juan Seguin walks up to Crockett.

SEGUIN
Look to the ridge, David.

(off Crockett)
You said you wanted to see him.

Crockett peers into the distance. Sure enough, Santa Anna and Batres approach a cannon placement on horseback.

CROCKETT
That's Santa Anna?

(off Seguin's nod)
Quite the peacock. Is he more politician or soldier?

SEGUIN
Whichever is appropriate at the time.

He smiles to Crockett, who smiles back, understanding that Seguin is speaking not only of Santa Anna.

SEGUIN (cont'd)
When General Iturbide betrayed the Fatherland he made himself emperor. So what did the young Santa Anna do to gain favor? He courted the emperor's sister.

CROCKETT
Heck, a man's got to get along in life. I was pretty ambitious as a young feller myself.

SEGUIN
She was sixty years old—

CROCKETT
I wasn't ever *that* ambitious.

EXT. FRONT LINES—CANNON PLACEMENT—DAY (CONTINUOUS)

Santa Anna and Batres arrive at Jesus's regiment, Santa Anna proudly reviewing his forces.

SANTA ANNA (Spanish)
(to the men)
It's a beautiful day. A beautiful day.

Santa Anna makes the men nervous. He spies Jesus, almost hiding behind the older men, summons him…

SANTA ANNA (Spanish) (cont'd)
Soldier!

(Jesus steps out; to Batres)
A boy fighting on the front, like a man.

(to Jesus)
You are very brave. I bet your grandfather fought the Comanches.

(Jesus nods)
And now your father is very proud of you, too.

JESUS (Spanish)
He is dead. He was hanged.

SANTA ANNA (Spanish)
Ah, murdered by the Gringos…

(gestures to Alamo)
I promise, you will have your revenge—

JESUS (Spanish)
He was hanged by you. At Orizaba. When you were fighting for the Spanish.

Everyone tenses. Santa Anna is slow to smile.

SANTA ANNA (Spanish)
We are Mexicans now, my friend, an honor for which we all will risk our lives many times.

Santa Anna turns, suddenly angry, fixating on the cannons.

SANTA ANNA (Spanish) (cont'd)
Why is this battery so far back?

The Battery Sergeant looks to the others, then steps forward.

BATTERY SERGEANT (Spanish)
Your Excellency, with respect, and for your safety… it is said that the Davy Crockett is in the Alamo.

(points to Alamo)
I have heard many stories of this great man. From my cousin.

SANTA ANNA (Spanish)
You are afraid of Crockett?!

Santa Anna dismounts and takes a few steps toward the Alamo. The Sergeant moves forward, trying to make his point to Santa Anna, who pauses.

BATTERY SERGEANT (Spanish)
It is said he can leap rivers—from there to here. And his rifle is accurate. He can shoot a fly off a burro's swishing tail at 200 yards.

Santa Anna looks at the man, shakes his head—"coward"—then strides toward the Alamo.

EXT. ALAMO WALL—DAY (CONTINUOUS)

Seguin watches as Crockett smiles, slowly lifts his rifle takes the ramrod from the muzzle.

AUTRY
(to Seguin)
I've seen him shoot the ant off an antelope at 600 feet.

A few other men gather around, sensing something important. Crockett's finger tenses on the trigger.

CROCKETT
That's it, Generalissimo, twenty more feet and I'll give ya a little peck on the cheek.

EXT. CANNON PLACEMENT—DAY (CONTINUOUS)

Santa Anna struts in front of the cannon placement. He digs his heels in the dirt, making a line—

SANTA ANNA (Spanish)
Move them to here!

EXT. PALISADE—DAY (CONTINUOUS)

Crockett takes a DEEP BREATH. Holds it. His finger squeezes—

EXT. CANNON PLACEMENT—DAY (CONTINUOUS)

Santa Anna is looking to the Alamo. On the wall, 600 feet away, a tiny puff of smoke—

The uniform on his shoulder TEARS OPEN. Santa Anna stumbles back, regains his composure and stares at the Alamo.

EXT. PALISADE—DAY (CONTINUOUS)

Crockett relaxes from the sniper position.

CROCKETT
Wind kicked up—

He tosses some dust in the air.

EXT. CANNON PLACEMENT—DAY (CONTINUOUS)

Santa Anna, now safely behind the cannon.

SANTA ANNA (Spanish)
Answer the pirates!

We watch as the Mexican soldiers start to load the cannon—ball, powder, fuse lit—and then—EVERYTHING GOES DARK—

AN EXPLOSION—and we're flying with the ball out of the tube over the landscape, clearing the wall of the Alamo and landing hard in—

EXT. ALAMO—COURTYARD—DAY (CONTINUOUS)

The middle of the courtyard and rolling to a stop. The men hit the deck, including Travis. The ball doesn't explode. It sits like a time bomb, the WICK STILL SPARKING.

Travis, getting to his feet, points to Ward.

TRAVIS
Get that shell and take it to Captain Dickinson.

Ward and the other men hesitate, look to Bowie and Crockett.

TRAVIS (cont'd)
We can reuse it.

Ward doesn't move. Sparks come off the ball.

WARD
You get it yourself.

Bowie and the men watch this direct disobedience. Travis stares down Ward as he walks to the shell, pulls out the burning wooden fuse, drops it on the ground and steps on it.

ARTILLERY PLATFORM

The men watch as Travis carries the shell to the 18-pounder.

TRAVIS
Captain Dickinson. Cut it to shot and give it back to them.

Dickinson nods, smiles.

TRAVIS (cont'd)
Fire the cannon.

Dickinson touches a light to the cannon. It FIRES. Nobody's saying anything, but Bowie is impressed with Travis, and his men, seeing him impressed, are impressed. Travis turns to the men below him.

TRAVIS (cont'd)
Fire once from each cannon!

There is a moment's hesitation among the men.

BOWIE
You heard the Colonel.

TRAVIS
Lt. Colonel... Colonel.

Bowie almost smiles...

BOWIE
You heard the man. Let's give 'em a taste.

Men cheer, race to their artillery posts, load and fire cannons—one, two, three cannons fire. Cannon fire becomes more cannon fire—mixed with Deguello—as we—

DISSOLVE TO:

EXT. ALAMO—NIGHT

The cannons FIRE down the line. BOOM. BOOM. BOOM. Men lie flat, long rifles visible.

INT. TRAVIS'S QUARTERS—NIGHT

Travis finishes another letter as Joe makes coffee. Seguin stands at the door.

TRAVIS
We have no idea if any of our couriers made it out. You know the land and the language.

SEGUIN
Colonel, you're asking me to leave my men behind.

TRAVIS
I'm asking you to deliver a message to Houston and return with a response. I'm counting on it.
(off Seguin's look)
I'm ordering it.

He holds the letter out. After a beat, Seguin takes it, walks away.

JOE
He comin' any day now ain't he, Mr. William? Colonel Fannin?

Travis turns to Joe, wishing he could lie—gives it a shot.

TRAVIS
Any day now, Joe. Any day.

EXT. ALAMO COURTYARD—MAIN GATE—NIGHT

Seguin finishes saddling a horse. Bowie leans in the doorway of his quarters alongside the main gate.

BOWIE
Don't give her too much water. She's just like me—drinks too much and she's not worth a damn.

SEGUIN
I will bring her back to you, Santiago.

BOWIE
Bring yourself back safe. Her, I don't think I'll be needing anymore.

Seguin mounts. Travis walks over.

TRAVIS
Tell Houston I'll fire a cannon at dawn, noon, and dusk each day our flag still flies. Go with God.

BOWIE
Ride like the devil.

Seguin WHISTLES DISTINCTIVELY to his men on the west wall.

SEGUIN (Spanish)
I'll see you soon, my friends!

Seguin watches the clouds until they cover the moon, then he waves and men on the north wall start firing their rifles and one cannon. A diversion.

Bowie slaps the horse's crup and Seguin races out the gate.

PALISADE

Crockett watches Seguin thread away in the night.

> BOWIE (O.S.)
> Makes a man ponder the possibilities, don't it?

Bowie slumps in the shadows at the end of the low barracks.

> BOWIE (cont'd)
> Even the great Davy Crockett.

> CROCKETT
> Yer kinda' famous, too.

> BOWIE
> (sits)
> Notorious. There's a difference.
> (eyes Crockett)
> Lose your fur cap?

> CROCKETT
> I just put it on when it's extra cold.
> (Bowie still stares)
> Truth is, I only started wearing that thing because of that feller in that play they did about me.
> (after a beat)
> People expect things.

> BOWIE
> Ain't it so.
> (after a beat; serious)
> Can I ask you something?

> CROCKETT
> All right.

> BOWIE
> Which was tougher... Jumping the Mississippi or riding a lightning bolt?

> CROCKETT
> (with a smile)
> Stories are like tadpoles. You turn your back and they've grown arms and legs and gone hoppin' all over creation.
> (an old complaint)
> And I tell you, I didn't make one cent off that book that feller wrote. If anyone ever tells you they wanna write you up, Jim, you make 'em pay you first.

A CANNON SHOT booms and hits the north wall opposite them. Brings their attention back to their situation...

> BOWIE
> Can you catch a cannon ball?

No smiles this time.

> CROCKETT
> If it was just simple old me, David, from Tennessee, I might drop over the wall some night and take my chances.
> (after a beat)
> But this Davy Crockett feller, they're all watching him. He's been fightin' on this wall every day of his life.

Bowie understands what Crockett is saying.

> BOWIE
> Sam Houston sent me down here to blow this fort up.
> (beat)
> I wish I had listened to him.

> CROCKETT
> I wish *I* hadn't.

They share a look. Bowie tries to rise, *collapses*.

INT. BOWIE'S QUARTERS—NIGHT

Bowie lies on a cot, burning up with fever. Juana uses a damp cloth on his face. Travis looks on, as do Crockett and Sam.

> JUANA
> He is burning with fever.

> TRAVIS
> Try to get him to drink something not whiskey.

> JUANA
> (to Sam)
> Bring me sheets and cold mud.

EXT. HILLTOP OUTSIDE OF TOWN—NIGHT

Seguin, now safe, stops his horse, looks back on the lights of Bexar and the Alamo—his hometown; his friends.

EXT. STREET OF SAN FELIPE—DAY

A few buildings are boarded up.

INT. PUBLIC BUILDING—DAY

The low-ceilinged, smoky, dark hall of politics. The point is nothing has changed. Burnet, Baker, Rusk, Smith, the same faces, same self-righteous expressions, same polarization.

> SMITH
> We have Mr. Thacher-Rhyme of the country of England...

Smith motions to an ENGLISHMAN, HAROLD THACHER-RHYME, 50.

> SMITH (cont'd)
> He represents interests willing to invest 5 million pounds in the new country of Texas—

> BURNET
> Need I remind anyone, for this soldier, the War of 1812 is very fresh in my mind.

Thacher-Rhyme can't believe these people.

> SMITH
> We must have resources to support our army and navy—

> BURNET
> Resources! Sir, at this very moment our soldiers are held in the Alamo against a force of thousands. They have put their hopes in Colonel Fannin, who despite his pedigree, has found himself ill-equipped to lead, much less march an army. In his letters he begs to be replaced. And there are other letters—

Burnet pulls a letter from his vest pocket—

> BURNET (cont'd)
> This from Colonel Travis...
> (reading)
> "I call on you in the name of Liberty, of patriotism and everything dear to the American character, to come to our aid with all dispatch.... If this call is neglected, I am determined to sustain myself as long as possible and die like a soldier who never forgets what is due to his own honor and that of his country—victory or death!"
> (beat)
> Can we allow these brave men to perish while we talk?
> (off their looks)
> We must fight! We must go to the Alamo!

HEAR-HEARS fill the room. A door SLAMS OPEN. Heads spin. There stands Sam Houston.

HOUSTON
I came to stop you people from killing yourselves, a service for which I feel certain I will never be properly thanked.

Burnet starts toward him. Houston raises his pistol.

HOUSTON *(cont'd)*
We can afford amateur military operations no longer—

BURNET
Are you slewed, Houston?

HOUSTON
We can afford amateur government no longer.

BURNET
Houston, you're raving drunk—

HOUSTON
You stripped me of my men to pillage a town of no military value 300 miles away.
(to Baker, Rusk, Burnet)
How did that work out for you? Where is the illustrious catamite, Dr. Grant? What has become of his conquering Matamoros party?

No one speaks.

HOUSTON *(cont'd)*
Dead. Gone to waste. We must not repeat the same mistake. We not only squander our lives, but the life of our country.
(beat)
I will raise an army. We will relieve the Alamo, but only when we have declared independence and created a government that can be legally recognized by the nations of the world. For that is what every besieged man in the Alamo is fighting for.

Thacher-Rhyme stands, can't help himself.

THACHER-RHYME
Finally. Good God. Listen to the man.

EXT. THE RIVER—DAY

A WOMAN washes her clothes then hears something, looks up to see a CAZADORE holding one finger to his lips—Shhh. Behind him, moving like silent death

through the woods are the Matamoros Permanentes, 100 strong. They double time, in formation, for the jacales near the southwest corner of the Alamo.

DANIEL CLOUD
Here they come, here they come!

IN THE COURTYARD we follow MEN as they run past the earthwork redoubt with cannons aimed at the gate, up onto the positions around the main gate.

Crockett and Tennesseans race up the southwest ramp to join—

EXT. ALAMO—SW RAMP—DAY

Travis and others. They stare at the odd formation just out of range. A moment of silence—two sides looking at one another. Then the soldiers double time into a new formation closer to the Alamo and line up to fire.

TRAVIS
Hold your fire. They're measuring our strength.

The Mexicans begin firing. Musket balls HIT around Travis. The MEN on the wall look at Travis like he's nuts.

TRAVIS *(cont'd)*
You may fire at will, gentlemen.

A VOLLEY from the Texians. Autry has loaded rifles next to him. He FIRES. A MEXICAN falls. He takes the next rifle. FIRES. A man falls.

We look down a line of long rifles, FIRING. Crockett strides on top of the wall, a big grin on his face.

CROCKETT
Make 'em count, boys, don't waste your powder—

A bullet HITS the wall a few inches from Crockett's foot.

CROCKETT *(cont'd)*
Pert near blew my bunions off.

Crockett aims. The SHOOTER appears. Crockett kills him.

Travis leaps to the 18-pounder, a musket ball PINGS off the barrel. Again, the men notice his bravery.

TRAVIS
Mr. Dickinson—

The cannon FIRES and, IN THE DISTANCE, one of the jacales splinters apart. The Mexicans flee back to their lines.

AUTRY
Lookit 'em go! Run, you rabbits!

The men CHEER. Crockett turns to Travis.

CROCKETT
Them little shacks offer pretty good cover.

TRAVIS
We can't waste more cannon shot.

CROCKETT
I wouldn't mind stretchin' my legs.

EXT. SOUTH WALL—DAY

SHARPSHOOTERS fall into position, taking aim. The main gate opens and Crockett and FOUR MEN exit with torches. Crockett walks toward the jacales, his MEN fanning out behind him.

AT THE JACALES

The men approach cautiously. Crockett in the lead, circles to the back of the first hut.

Crockett lights the straw roof. He hears a NOISE. Two Mexican SOLDIERS burst through the flaming door, firing their weapons. One musket EXPLODES in the hands of the soldier.

The other FIRES and the ball barely misses Crockett's hip. He looks down, not quite believing he's not dead. He fires his own weapon, killing the man instantly. The other soldier draws his sword. Crockett draws a knife.

As the soldier SWINGS the blade, a hole opens in his chest. Surprised, he falls to his knees.

A CHEER FROM THE WALL as Travis lowers a rifle and hands it back to its owner.

The jacales are now a bonfire. The men return to the Alamo. Crockett pauses a beat hears something—

A WOUNDED CAZADORE—still alive in the grass, gutshot, trying to get powder into his Baker rifle. He sees Crockett, drops the gun and begins slowly, painfully dragging himself backwards through the grass.

Crockett follows him. The Mexican stops, looks back at Crockett.

Crockett SHEATHS his knife, kneels down, and looks at the young man.

CROCKETT
What's your name, son?

The soldado dies before Crockett's eyes. Crockett stares at his face, momentarily lost. Then he picks up the rifle lying on the ground, shoulders it.

CROCKETT (cont'd)
Muchos Gracias.

Crockett turns and follows the others through the high grass.

EXT. ALAMO SOUTH WALL—DAY

The men WHOOP as Crockett enters the gate. Still in shock he nods and accepts slaps on the back. He spots Travis and gives him a nod of thanks. Travis spots Sam on the other side of the yard —

SAM
Colonel Travis! Colonel Travis!

And makes his way toward Bowie's quarters.

INT. BOWIE'S QUARTERS—DAY

Bowie SHOUTS, MOANS, delirious. He foams at the mouth. His eyes open but he is seeing nothing. He thrashes around. Travis and Sam try to hold him.

BOWIE
Oh, no, please God—my baby— our baby!! Ursula!

In a fever fit, Bowie wraps his hands around Travis's neck. Sam pulls them away and Juana steps in to help. Finally Bowie relaxes. Sam and a shocked Travis step back from the bed.

SAM
He's been crying for her all day.

TRAVIS
Who?

SAM
His wife, and the baby she carried. Dead from cholera.

EXT. BOWIE'S QUARTERS—DAY

As Travis exits he finds FIFTY OR SIXTY VOLUNTEERS standing in ragtag formation. Travis is on guard, half-expecting mutiny. Ward stands in front of them.

WARD
Is he gonna get better?

TRAVIS
I don't know.

Ward is blocking his way.

WARD
Up there on that wall, we killed six Mexicans and lost nary a man.

A beat where they stare at each other.

WARD (cont'd)
We can take 'em.

Ward looks at the other men. A movement ripples through as they come to a sort of attention. Even Ward straightens up.

WARD (cont'd)
We can take 'em, Sir.

PANNING the faces of the men. They want to believe and they look to him to reinforce that belief. Travis's face says that maybe for the first time he understands what leadership is.

INT. PUBLIC BUILDING—NIGHT

WOMEN sew the TEXAS FLAG. Rusk and others draft a Declaration of Independence. Houston walks to a map on a wall. He traces from Copano to Refugio, Goliad to Victoria, and, finally, Gonzalez.

HOUSTON
I have ordered Colonel Fannin to retreat from Goliad to Gonzalez. John Forbes is mustering more men throughout South Texas and bringing them to Gonzalez. I expect 1,500 men to be there when I arrive. We will ford Olmos Creek upstream from Bexar, relieve the Alamo from the west then withdraw to Gonzalez and fortify in a line southeast to Columbus and Brazoria.

The room is beginning to BUZZ in favor of Houston.

BURNET
You'll have command of the regular army. The militias will have their own command.

HOUSTON
No.
(challenging the room)
I will have command of all or none.

Houston strides to the table where the constitution is still being worked on. He scribbles SAM HOUSTON on the bottom.

HOUSTON (cont'd)
Finish this government. Do your calling and I shall do mine. I will lead an army. You will birth a nation.
(beat)
Gentlemen, again, to Texas!

The men give a hearty HEAR-HEAR. Thacher-Rhyme seems pleased. Burnet catches Houston on his way to the door.

BURNET
Houston, if I hear of you drunk, it's over. You will never have an official role in Texas again.

EXT. STREET—SAN FELIPE—NIGHT

Houston finishes packing a saddle bag, looks at a bottle of whiskey, considers, then realizes Mathew Ingram, ridiculously hopeful, is watching him. After a beat—

HOUSTON
You have a horse?

MATHEW
Yep.

HOUSTON
How about a gun?

MATHEW
I can find one.

Houston assesses the teenager. He takes a last glance at the bottle, SMASHES it.

HOUSTON
Well, go get 'em.

We hear a BUGLE playing a tune we haven't heard before—

ESPARZA (V.O.)
The bugles signals the arrival of reinforcements.

THROUGH FIELD GLASS—more Mexican troops pour into Bexar.

EXT. ALAMO WEST WALL—DAY

Gregorio Esparza stands beside Travis intently listening to the TRUMPETS. It's clear he understands the signals.

TRAVIS
How many?

Esparza really doesn't want to tell Travis.

ESPARZA
Three more battalions. A thousand more soldados.

TRAVIS
(after a beat)
At least now we know what they were waiting for.

ESPARZA
(points)
Over there—what are they working at?

THROUGH THE GLASSES—dozens of
Mexican soldiers on their hands and
knees building something. Only when
they stand and lift do we see what they
have constructed. LADDERS.

Travis lowers the glasses, sighs.

MEN ON THE WALL

They stare at the ladders, all thinking the
same thing.

SCURLOCK makes a mark on the top of
the wall with his knife—TEN MARKS,
TEN DAYS. He stares at the mark, looks
up to the ladders being built and carried.

SCURLOCK
We're all gonna die.

INT. COURTYARD—DAY

A few men, including Crockett and Autry,
pile trunks near the church—a makeshift
breastworks.

At the well, Sam and Joe have dug deep
enough that they are well below ground
and can converse in private.

SAM
When they come over these
walls, you just throw up you
hands and holler "Soy Negro, no
disparo!"

JOE
What's that?

SAM
Mexican law says there ain't no
slaves, right? An' contrack or no
that's what you is. Mexicans see
your color, you tell 'em not to
shoot, and they'll pass you by.

JOE
Mr. William gonna give me a
gun.

SAM
You clean up they shit, take care
of they horses, wash 'em, feed
'em. Damn if you ain't gonna die
for 'em, too.

Joe looks down at his hands, which are
cracked and blistered. The shovel bites
the earth, stops.

JOE
How do you say them words,
again?

INT. LONG BARRACKS—DAY

New Orleans Greys dig a trench in the
ground—a fallback position. Grey #1
stops for a moment, wipes his brow.

GREY #1
Dig 'er deep boys. Always good
to have a fall-back position.

GREY #2
About the size of a grave, ain't it,
Captain?

EXT. ALAMO SW BATTERY—DAY

Travis and Dickinson…

TRAVIS
Captain Dickinson, I'm re-assign-
ing you and Private Esparza to
the battery in the rear of the
church so you can be near your
families.
(off Dickinson's look)
And I've arranged for a replace-
ment for your midnight watch.

Dickinson nods, knowing Travis is
preparing for the worst. Travis exits the
ramp and is met by BONHAM.

BONHAM
Colonel?
(off Travis's look)
Some of the men are uncertain
about the loyalties of the Tejano
you sent for help.

TRAVIS
Colonel Bowie has absolute faith
in Captain Seguin.

BONHAM
Perhaps, then, he just didn't
make it.
(off Travis)
I'd like to give it a shot.

Travis gives Bonham a biting smile, then
walks away.

BONHAM *(cont'd)*
Billy!
(Travis stops, turns)
That look you just gave me is
exactly why people didn't like
you growing up. If you think I
just want out of here, you're
wrong.

TRAVIS
(after a beat)
I can't afford another man, particularly another good man.

(off Bonham)
I've sent fourteen messengers out
since we retreated to this fort. No
one has come back.

Bonham and Travis share a look. Bonham's says, "But you haven't sent me."

EXT. ALAMO GATE—NIGHT

The gates open. Bonham jumps on his
horse, touches his hat, a gesture to Travis.

TRAVIS
Go with God.

Bonham rides away.

INT. BOWIE'S QUARTERS—NIGHT

Bowie's eyes are open. He is drenched in
sweat. Juana arranges an altar of candles
and plaster saints, at the center, a cameo
of Ursula.

Ana Esparza passes a chicken egg in circles over Bowie's forehead, heart, and
intestines. Sam watches from outside the
doorway.

JUANA
He has been stabbed, three
times, once through the lungs,
shot two or three times, cholera,
and malaria, every two years.

Ana cracks the egg into a glass, looks at
it.

ANA
He is already dead… and this is
the place he's been sent.

The yolk has a red spot in the center.
Juana crosses herself and leaves. Bowie
shifts, groans, calls out for his dead wife.
His eyes open and—

She's there—Ursula sits before him, in
her wedding gown. Bowie reaches for
"Ursula." Juana takes his hand, then leans
down and kisses him on the lips, quiet-
ing him.

INT. YTURRI HOUSE—NIGHT

A GOLD CROSS sits in front of Santa
Anna, who stands next to the stunning
Tejana girl. A wedding ceremony is in
progress. We see the girl's mother standing beside Mexican generals.

CASTRILLÓN (Spanish)
(whispers to Cos)
What do you think your sister
will say when she hears?

COS (Spanish)
("not from me")
Hear from who?

WORDS are spoken and only then do we see that the "priest" is Batres, in religious attire. And then WE HEAR MUSIC and the din of celebration, which carries with the wind to—

EXT. WEST WALL—NIGHT

Scurlock and others, including Grimes.

SCURLOCK
What the hell are they celebrating?

GRIMES
A rout.

NORTH END OF THE COURTYARD

The men are exhausted, dirty. They dip corn tortillas into plates of stew.

DANIEL CLOUD
In all your Indian fighting, you must have been in a scrape like this.

CROCKETT
I wasn't ever in but one real scrape in my life, fellas.

Cloud looks at him in disbelief. Joe, carrying a clay pot filled with stew, refills plates.

DANIEL CLOUD
You was in the Red Stick War.

CROCKETT
Yeah, that's true. I was in that. I was just about your age when it broke out. The Creeks boxed up four, five hundred people at Fort Nims and massacred every one of 'em. This was big news around those parts, so I up and joined the volunteers.

Other men move in close to hear.

CROCKETT (cont'd)
I did a little scoutin', but mostly I fetched in venison for the cook-fire. Well, we caught up with them redskins at Tallusahatchee. We surrounded the whole village and come in from all directions. It wasn't much of a fight, really. We shot them down like dogs...

SENTRIES on the wall peering down to listen, not watching their posts. Crockett has the men in the palm of his hand.

CROCKETT (cont'd)
Finally, what was left of them injuns crowded into this little cabin. They wanted to surrender, but this squaw loosed an arrow and killed one of the fellas, so we shot her and then... Then, we set fire to the cabin. We could hear 'em screaming to their gods in there. We could smell 'em.

Crockett puts down his plate of stew.

CROCKETT (cont'd)
We had had nary to eat but parched corn since October and that was near gone. The next day when we dug through the ashes we found these potaters from the cellar. They'd been cooked by the grease that run off them Indians. We ate 'til we near burst.

We PAN ACROSS the rapt faces of the men.

CROCKETT (cont'd)
Since then, you pass me the taters, I'll pass 'em right back.

The message settles in on the faces of the men. A GUNSHOT breaks the moment.

SCURLOCK
I think I hit one of 'em!

All over the Alamo men are SCRAMBLING to positions. From below Scurlock comes a man BITCHING.

COLORADO SMITH (O.S.)
(muffled)
Son of a goddamned shit-arse bitch! What do I look like, you blind turd?

GRIMES
I think they're talkin' American.

COLORADO SMITH (O.S.)
(muffled)
Open the gate! It's us!

EXT. ALAMO MAIN GATE—NIGHT (CONTINUOUS)

The gate is opened and armed MEN on horseback, led by Colorado Smith, enter. There is a WHOOP from the defenders.

MICAJAH AUTRY
They're here! Reinforcements! They're here!

Crockett and the Tennesseans race over, joined by others.

EXT. ALAMO—COURTYARD—NIGHT

Colorado Smith dismounts and gives Travis a salute.

COLORADO SMITH
(proudly)
I figure this is every able-bodied man in Gonzales.

Most of the men gather around, shaking hands and slapping backs as NEWCOMERS dismount.

COLORADO SMITH (cont'd)
Those soldados think they got it all sewn up tight, but you avoid the roads, there's this little sliver you can ease on through.

TRAVIS
And Colonel Fannin is behind you?

COLORADO SMITH
He ain't here? I talked to him three days ago in Goliad. The sonofabitch said he was coming.

TRAVIS
How many rode with you?

COLORADO SMITH
I brung thirty-two men, Colonel.

Travis turns away to conceal his disappointment. Crockett sees the dejected faces of his comrades.

CROCKETT
And if they ain't the purtiest lookin' bunch of Texians I ever seen. Let's hear it for Gonzales, fellas—

The Tennesseans give a CHEER. Others join. More CHEERING. We notice that Dickinson tries to smile, but can't, his disappointment palpable.

INT. YTURRI HOUSE—NIGHT

As the remains of the wedding party is cleaned in the background Santa Anna, Castrillón, and Almonte stand at the window facing the Alamo. Santa Anna hears the faint CHEERING drifting from the fort.

SANTA ANNA (Spanish)
It is not Houston who has arrived?

ALMONTE (Spanish)
No. A few men on horseback, that's all.

SANTA ANNA (Spanish)
I leave a corridor wide open for him, here, come here, come to

us, bring your army, your opportunity to be a great Gringo hero.... Still, he doesn't come. What can I do?

No answer. He walks away, has a thought.

SANTA ANNA (Spanish) *(cont'd)*
Send a message that we grant safe quarter to any Tejano choosing to leave the Alamo. They will take their freedom and the men left behind will think about escape, about life, and they will not fight like men resigned to death.

INT. CHURCH—BAPTISTRY—NIGHT

Dickinson looks down on his wife and baby, lying on the floor. He walks over, lies down beside them, holds them.

INT. YTURRI HOUSE—NIGHT

Santa Anna walks to his bedroom door, opens it. Inside, his girl "bride" sits on the bed, in night clothes, terrified.

Santa Anna smiles, steps inside and closes the door—shutting us out from his "wedding" night.

EXT. GRASSLANDS—DAY

Houston and Mathew ride along.

MATHEW
When do you think we'll see action?

HOUSTON
Don't know.

MATHEW
Do you think we'll fight Indians, too?

HOUSTON
Don't know.

MATHEW
I bet you hadn't seen action by the time you were my age.

HOUSTON
Can't remember.

MATHEW
You were probably in school. Probably doing what you were supposed to be doing.

HOUSTON
Probably.

MATHEW
Really?

HOUSTON
My two brothers were teachers, the apostles. I loved to learn but if anyone could remove the joy from something, it was the apostles. I ran away and lived with the Cherokees.

MATHEW
I'm running away right now, but maybe I'll kill Santa Anna.

(off Houston)
My Pa says I'm idle and lazy, but I'm not anymore. I'm reformed.

This causes Houston to SNORT out a laugh.

HOUSTON
You and me.

They round a bend and DOWN BELOW see the Gonzalez "ARMY," a handful of tents and a few men.

MATHEW
Did you ever see so many people in all your life?

Houston just stares—

EXT. CAMP—DAY

Houston with Mosely Baker, J.C. Neill, OTHERS outside a tent.

HOUSTON
Where is everybody?

NEILL
Thirty men from here in Gonzalez already left for the Alamo.

Off to the side, a YOUNG MAN WITH A fife in his pocket—

FIFER
General, my brother and four real good men are on their way from Brazoria.

Houston looks around, sees the sorry state of things.

HOUSTON
Assemble them.

A WOMAN, 50s—MRS. MILLSAPS, stands in the crowd.

MRS. MILLSAPS
I need to talk to him. I need to talk to General Sam Houston!

HOUSTON
I'm Houston.

He nods and she is led over. Houston is taken aback by the sight of the woman. She's blind.

MRS. MILLSAPS
God bless you, sir. My husband's there. At the Alamo. He said it was his duty. To go, to try and save those poor men. And I understand that, I do. We have six children and they cry for their daddy. But today I told them that you had come and that you were going there. To bring him back. To bring them all back. And I just wanted to meet you, to thank you. God bless you, sir.

Houston, dumbstruck, just watches as she's led away. Houston hears a DISTINCTIVE WHISTLE, turns to see—

Juan Seguin ride up and come to a halt. He jumps down off his horse and shares a look with Houston. Two warriors.

HOUSTON (V.O.)
How many in the Alamo?

EXT. GONZALEZ CAMP—DAY

Seguin follows Houston as he looks over the assembled troops, Mathew included, staring into the face of each man they pass. Men who are dusty, buck-skinned, some wearing sombreros...

SEGUIN
One hundred and fifty. Not counting women and children.

Houston stops, taken aback.

HOUSTON
Women and children?

Seguin nods. Houston sighs but keeps looking at the troops.

HOUSTON *(cont'd)*
If Bowie had just done what I asked...

SEGUIN
Santiago is not well, General.

(off Houston's look)
But morale is good. Travis has lost some of his rough edges and Crockett keeps the men amused—

HOUSTON
(stops cold)
Crockett? Crockett's there?

SEGUIN
With a group of your fellow Tennesseans.

The news stuns Houston. He seems a bit lost, then he walks away from the troops, from Seguin. Mosely Baker and J.C. Neill watch as Houston walks out into the field, alone. Then he bends down to his knees and puts his head to the ground— distant SOUNDS OF CANNON FIRE.

MOSELY BAKER
When we moving out?

Houston stands to find Baker and Billingsley behind him. He looks past them to the assembled men.

HOUSTON
We need more men, stronger men, younger men. If they arrive every day, soon we will have enough, but for now, we wait.

Baker and Neill can't believe their ears.

MOSELY BAKER
If we can't run, we walk. If we can't walk, we crawl, but we must go to the aid of those boys! It's only right!

NEILL
General, I'm the man who left Travis there!

HOUSTON
And I'm the man who sent him.
  (angry)
I do not enjoy waiting any more than the next man but I will not sacrifice Texas!

  (softens a bit; eyes the troops)
These 124 men cannot pierce an army of thousands.

The officers look at one another. They realize this math means they aren't ever going.

HOUSTON *(cont'd)*
Colonel Fannin is enroute from Goliad with 400 men. These troops need training. I suggest you commence with that.

Houston walks away. He is joined by Seguin...

SEGUIN
What should I tell Travis?

HOUSTON
Nothing. You're staying here.

SEGUIN
No, General,... Sam,... I gave my word.

HOUSTON
That's an order.

Houston walks away. Baker whips off his hat and throws it down in disgust.

EXT. ALAMO COURTYARD—DAY
The faces of Seguin's men, as a group look upon—a group of civilian Tejanos, packed to leave, saying good-bye to loved ones. Gregorio Esparza and his family are staying.

INT. BOWIE'S QUARTERS—DAY
Bowie is lucid. Juana sits over him, Sam stands nearby.

JUANA
You look better. Your fever broke.

BOWIE
Thank you for tending to me. And now I want you to leave. You, too, Sam.

SAM
  (amazed)
You giving me my papers, Mr. James?

BOWIE
No. You are my property 'til I die. I get off my back, I'm gonna come fetch you.

  (off their looks)
Now go, both of you. Santa Anna won't make the same offer twice.

Sam trades one last look with Bowie, then leaves. Juana stays. Bowie gives her a hard look.

JUANA
No. We're family.

BOWIE
A couple of years doesn't make us blood, Juana.

JUANA
You loved her. Her blood was yours. Your blood is mine.

Bowie turns away—remembering his loss.

EXT. ALAMO COURTYARD—DAY
Texians watch a group of TEJANOS pass through the open gate, pulling their horses and carrying their belongings.

We LOOK CLOSER and see that SAM, wearing a sombrero and serape, is among them. He keeps his head down. In fact, none of the Tejanos make eye-contact as they leave.

Ana, Juana, Gregorio, and other Tejanos watching them go. The gate closes behind them, sealing in those who remain.

EXT. HILLS OUTSIDE BEXAR—DAY
A lone HORSEMAN gallops up a hill. Bonham—with a white bandanna on his hat. He starts forward, then back, forward, then back. Getting up his nerve. When we see what he sees—the Mexican forces between him and the Alamo—we know why. He grimaces, spurs his horse down the hill, toward an impenetrable cordon.

EXT. REAR MEXICAN LINES—DAY
Mr. Bonham's wild ride. He blasts past soldiers sitting by cook fires, leaps over hedges, lowers his body down so he's hugging the neck of the horse and holds on.

SOLDIERS figuring out what's going on, run toward him, kneel, aiming, FIRE, missing. Balls WHISTLE past Bonham's head.

EXT. WALL—DAY
The men begin gathering along the side. They crane to see. IN THE DISTANCE, Bonham, now chased by MOUNTED LANCERS, gallops straight toward them.

Crockett FIRES, the lead lancer drops. Crockett is passed another rifle. He FIRES. A horse falls and the lancers give up the chase.

BELOW men open the gate and Bonham gallops in. As Bonham dismounts, the men watch him nervously.

WARD
You don't have 2,000 more just like you stashed away somewheres, do you?

SCURLOCK
When they comin'?! When the hell they comin'?!

BONHAM
Where is Colonel Travis?

INT. TRAVIS HEADQUARTERS—DAY
Joe and Bonham watch Travis read a letter, toss it down.

TRAVIS
Where did you get these?

BONHAM
I crossed two of our couriers on the way back.

Travis looks at Bonham, beginning to understand.

TRAVIS
Afraid to return.
(off Bonham's look)
And where is your letter? What says Colonel Fannin?

Bonham just shakes his head. The weight of this sinks in. After a beat, Travis looks at Bonham, a bit overcome.

TRAVIS *(cont'd)*
Captain Bonham, you rode through the possibility of death to deliver a message that promises it. Why?...

BONHAM
I believe you have earned the pleasure of a reply... Sir.

Travis slowly nods a "thank you." Bonham nods and leaves.

EXT. COURTYARD—DAY

The men are gathered in a large group.

SCURLOCK
I say we run for it. That's our best hope.

THE CROWD
Yeah. Damn right.

WARD
Our horses are starving and weak. Their lancers would skewer us like sausages.

GRIMES
Our relief could be over that hill—

GREY #2
We could go out at night. In formation, some would make it.

GRIMES
We could try surrendering.

Some in the crowd HISS, but some are willing to consider it.

SCURLOCK
Check if that red flag is still flying.

Crockett is listening from the back of the group.

INT. TRAVIS'S HEADQUARTERS—DAY

Travis is showing Joe how to work a rifle. Crockett enters.

CROCKETT
The men need a word from you.

Travis is stretched thin. He gathers his thoughts slowly.

TRAVIS
I... I don't know what to tell them.

Crockett ponders this a moment.

CROCKETT
My time in Washington—the fellas in Congress made a good deal of sport of me. I learned a lot from them—learned how to dress, to a certain degree, what fork to use in polite company, things of that nature. And I've never been afraid to stretch the truth a bit, but... I never learned to lie.

Travis looks out at the men in the fort.

CROCKETT *(cont'd)*
These people in here been through an awful lot. I would allow these men have earned the right to hear the truth.

EXT. ALAMO—COURTYARD—DAY

A raised hand holds pieces of paper. Travis faces his men.

TRAVIS
I have here pieces of paper, letters from politicians and generals, but no indication of when or if help will arrive. Letters not worth the ink committed to them.
(after a beat)
I fear that... no one is coming.

He slowly crumples the letters, drops them to the earth. He looks at incredible mix of peoples assembled: Irish, German, Tejano, young, old, educated, ignorant.

TRAVIS *(cont'd)*
Texas has been a second chance for me. I expect that might be true for many of you men. It has been a chance not only for land and riches, but also to be a different man, hopefully a better man.
(a beat)
There have been many ideas brought forth in the last few

months of what Texas is, of what it should become.
(looks to Tejanos)
We are not all in agreement.
(another beat)
I'd like each of you men to think of what it is you value so highly that you are willing to fight and possibly to die for it. We will call that Texas.

Travis looks into the eyes of his men.

TRAVIS *(cont'd)*
The Mexican army hopes to lure us into attempting escape.... Almost anything seems better than remaining in this place, penned up.
(beat)
But, what about our wounded? What about the sick? In the open, without our cannon, they will cut us to pieces. We will have deserted our injured and died in vain. If, however, we force the enemy to attack, I believe every one of you will prove himself worth ten in return. We will not only show the world what patriots are made of, but we will also deal a crippling blow to the army of Santa Anna.
(beat)
If anyone wishes to depart, under the white flag of surrender, you may do so now. You have that right. But if you wish to stay with me, here, in the Alamo, we will sell our lives dearly.

Nobody speaks. Nobody moves. Joe, looking on, wells with a bit of pride. Travis waits a beat, realizes that the troops are with him, then walks away, through them, toward his quarters. Once he's *inside*... he looks out the window at the men, still staring at him, closes the shutters and sighs.

INT. BOWIE'S QUARTERS—LATER—DAY

Bowie, on his side, retching over a bowl, looks up, sees Travis standing respectfully in the doorway. As Travis starts to close the door...

BOWIE
Leave it. The light. I want the light.
(after a beat)
What troubles you, Buck?

TRAVIS
I spoke to the men earlier. About our situation. You deserve to hear as well.

BOWIE
I heard. Through the door. Every word.

TRAVIS
(sits, with a sly smile)
My words. How painful for you.

BOWIE
Good words.

TRAVIS
We could try to get you out. With an escort. If you are captured, perhaps, given your condition, mercy would be extended.

BOWIE
I don't deserve mercy.
(after a beat)
But I do deserve a drink. You have anything stronger than water?

TRAVIS
I don't drink, Jim. You know that.
(beat)
I gamble. Go to whores. Run off on wives, but drinking... I draw the line.

BOWIE
You know, Buck, if you live another five years, you might be a great man.

TRAVIS
I think I'll probably have to settle for what I am now.

Travis slowly stands, moves for the door.

BOWIE
Buck?...

Travis stops, turns.

BOWIE *(cont'd)*
Did it matter?...

A moment between the two men as they consider their fate.

TRAVIS
(after a beat)
I'll see about fetching you a bottle.

Travis leaves, closing the door behind him.

EXT. ALAMO—PALISADE—DUSK

Deguello begins. Autry sighs, prepares for the barrage.

AUTRY
God, I despise that tune.

Crockett listens, then smiles.

CROCKETT
Just figgered it out.

AUTRY
Figured out what?

He reaches in his bag, grabs his fiddle and scurries away...

CROCKETT
What it's missing.

ATOP THE MAIN GATE BUILDING

Crockett raises his fiddle and starts to accompany the distant trumpets, providing harmony.

EXT. MEXICAN CANNON PLACEMENT—NIGHT

Jesus and the others hear the fiddle, smile.

BATTERY SERGEANT
(grins to men)
Croque...

EXT. ALAMO WALLS—NIGHT

At this moment in time there is no siege, no battle, no war, just music floating through the air. We see the faces of the men as, for a moment, they are peaceful.

ATOP THE MAIN GATE BUILDING

The song ends. Crockett lowers his fiddle—

CROCKETT
Amazing what a little harmony will do, ain't it?

And waits, along with the others, for the barrage to come. But strangely—*It doesn't.*

VARIOUS SHOTS

Defenders slowly pull their fingers from their ears, rise and stare. No cannons will be fired tonight.

FORSYTH
Well, if that isn't something.

EXT. ALAMO—VARIOUS SHOTS—NIGHT

WE MOVE ALONG THE MEN, writing final letters. ISAAC MILLSAPS—one of the Gonzales men, sits in a corner and scrawls.

MILLSAPS (V.O.)
Dearest Mary, I hope someone with a kind voice is reading this to you. If you could see, you'd know how beautiful this land, our home is. Kiss all six children for me, and kiss them again....

BONHAM re-reads his before he sticks it in an envelope.

BONHAM (V.O.)
Please remember me to my father and tell him to think of nothing but of coming here to this fair country when it is free....

WARD, on the north wall, stares into the night....

WARD (V.O.)
We know what awaits us, and we are prepared to meet it....

INT. TRAVIS QUARTERS—NIGHT (CONTINUOUS)

Joe watches as Travis stares at a page—halfway through a letter.

JAMES ALLEN
Sir?...

James Allen stands in the doorway, a satchel around his neck, a handful of letters in his hand.

JAMES ALLEN *(cont'd)*
I've gathered the men's letters.

TRAVIS
Spare me a moment more?

Smith nods, walks away. Travis puts his pen to paper

TRAVIS (V.O.) *(cont'd)*
Take care of my little boy....

Writing these words gives Travis pause. He wells up, fights tears...

INT. BOWIE'S QUARTERS—NIGHT

We move past several men praying, thinking, find Crockett through Bowie's doorway, sitting, entertaining Bowie, who lies on the bed, in bad shape.

CROCKETT
There was this feller from London, England. Wore dandy britches. He made a voice come out of his pocket, then he put it in my pocket.

Crockett looks down at his pocket and works the flaps like a little mouth—

CROCKETT (cont'd)
(voice from pocket)
Hello… Hello… I'm trapped in your pocket. I liked to jump right out of my socks. And then he had him a moon-faced doll, mean as ten hornets, wearing a tricorn hat. She was real as you or me.
(looking at his hand)
Hello. Hello. You're that Crockett feller, ain't ye?

The two men share a laugh. Then Crockett's smile drops. He picks up Bowie's pistols, checks their powder.

CROCKETT (cont'd)
I rode on a steam train. I rode on a steam boat. I'd trade all them memories for five more minutes of that doll in the tricorn hat.

The two men, now friends, share a knowing smile. Then…

BOWIE
Help me up.

Crockett helps Bowie into a sitting position on the bed. The two men stare at one another.

BOWIE (cont'd)
Am I up?

CROCKETT
Yes you are.

BOWIE
They'll come from all sides to keep you occupied but the real attack will be focused on one wall. My bet—the north. Hold your wits and always keep one eye behind you.

Crockett looks up at Bowie, who shakes his head ever so slightly.

BOWIE (cont'd)
You don't need me any more than you need that cap. You been on these walls every day of your life.
(off Crockett's look)
Would you help me with my vest?

Crockett spots Bowie's vest beside the bed, and helps lift Bowie's arms into it. Bowie lies back down.

Crockett half-cocks the pistols and sets them beside Bowie's legs, helping Bowie's hands find triggers. The two

share one last look before Crockett leaves, closing the door behind him.

INT. YTURRI HOUSE—NIGHT

Santa Anna and his generals surround the big table, look at a map and discuss strategy. Santa Anna eats dinner and references the map as he speaks.

SANTA ANNA (Spanish)
General Cos, you will be given opportunity to redeem yourself.

COS (Spanish)
Thank you, your Excellency.

SANTA ANNA (Spanish)
You will lead the first charge. Here at the weak north wall.

Cos's face says this is a tough assignment.

SANTA ANNA (Spanish) (cont'd)
Colonel Duque will follow—from the northeast. Romero, from the east. Morales—south. General Ramirez y Sesma, your cavalry will insure that no one escapes or retreats.

Castrillón has been listening, biting his tongue. Finally…

CASTRILLÓN (Spanish)
Excellency, our 12-pound cannon arrives tomorrow. Why risk the lives of so many of our own who will die trying to take a wall that can be demolished?

Santa Anna looks at his dinner plate.

SANTA ANNA (Spanish)
What are the lives of soldiers… but so many chickens?

CASTRILLÓN (Spanish)
And if they surrender?

SANTA ANNA (Spanish)
They are pirates, not soldiers. No prisoners.

CASTRILLÓN (Spanish)
Your Excellency, there are rules governing—

SANTA ANNA (Spanish)
I am governing! And, you, Sir, have no understanding of the difficulties that entails!

This is the first time we've seen Santa Anna really angry. He faces off with Castrillón. He needs them to understand…

SANTA ANNA (Spanish) (cont'd)
I am committed to giving our country a national identity. Did we gain independence only to let our land be stolen from us? It stops here. It must. For if it doesn't our grandchildren and their grandchildren will suffer the disgrace of one day begging for crumbs from the Gringo.
(after a beat)
Without blood, without tears, there is no glory.

Castrillón realizes the die is cast.

EXT. ALAMO—WALLS—NIGHT

We TRACK PAST several Texians, exhausted, sprawled next to their loaded rifles on the parapet, dead asleep.

EXT. MEXICAN CAMP—NIGHT

Jesus is quietly wakened by the Sergeant. Soldiers are preparing for battle: tightening belts, loading weapons, kneeling for last prayers, all without uttering a word.

EXT. PLAINS AROUND ALAMO—NIGHT

All we see is high grass and some rustling. And then, out of the grass, a column of soldiers rises. They move forward silently, on cat's paws.

EXT. ALAMO—COS COLUMN—NIGHT

Jesus falls into step with the hundreds of men, led by General Cos, quietly approaching the fort from the north.

INT. ALAMO CHAPEL—MEN—NIGHT

The Tennesseans are all sleeping, except for Crockett, who sits, fiddle in his lap, staring straight ahead. With one finger he plucks a string, stops—does he hear something?…

EXT. ALAMO—MEXICAN POSITIONS—NIGHT

Colonel Duque's COLUMN, 400 strong, with ladders, peel off and head for the center of the north wall.

EXT. ALAMO—NORTHEAST—NIGHT

Three hundred RIFLEMEN under Colonel Romero carry ladders toward the low walls of the cattle pen.

EXT. ALAMO—SOUTH—NIGHT

One hundred RIFLEMEN under Morales move from the south toward the low palisade. As they reach the Abatis they start to creep forward, moving ever closer to the palisade wall.

We see feet marching silently, in boots, shoes, sandals. The shadows of a multitude of soldiers move across the ground. We TILT UP—the Alamo walls loom closer.

EXT. ALAMO SENTRY POSITION—NIGHT

Grimes sleeps in a little dug-out position twenty yards from the Alamo walls. A hand covers his mouth, his eyes pop open as a bayonet is rammed into his chest.

AT THE PALISADE

Crockett hears something, slowly sets down his fiddle, grabs his rifle walks to the fence, steps up to see over and —

Is face to face with a soldado less than five feet away. Both are shocked to see the other but Crockett reacts first, shooting the soldier just as —

NORTH WALL

Jesus is terrified. Beside him, a nervous soldier can't contain himself—

JOSE TORRES (Spanish)
Long live Santa Anna!

Another voice calls out from Duque's column to the left.

VOICE (O.S.) (Spanish)
Long live the Republic!

Suddenly, MEN are YELLING from all sides and RUNNING, Jesus swept up as they break ranks and charge the walls.

INT. TRAVIS'S ROOM—NIGHT

Travis jumps from his bed, Joe leaps off his cot, both grabbing a weapon and rushing out.

EXT. ALAMO COURTYARD—NIGHT

Travis passes Bonham and they share a look before Travis races toward the north wall—

TRAVIS
Come on, boys! The Mexicans are upon us!

Bonham, Dickinson and the rest of the crew wake and spring up behind their cannons on the chapel platform.

Crockett and his men fire at the palisade.

Texians come sprinting out of the long barracks, rifles in hand, spreading out in four directions to their stations.

EXT. ALAMO—COS COLUMN—NIGHT

Jesus runs toward the wall, closer, closer—BLAM! SCREAMS as the first ROUND of CANISTER SHOT rips through the tightly packed militiamen, Jesus sprayed with blood as men all around him go down.

More men fall as the Texian RIFLES begin to take their toll. Jesus is swept back as men in front of him turn to run but there officers flail at the men with their staffs and flat swords, driving them toward the wall.

SARGENTO (Spanish)
Charge. . . . Charge!

EXT. ALAMO—CHURCH PLATFORM—NIGHT

We look past the CANNONS as BOOM! BOOM! BOOM! They FIRE down into the Romero column, the front lines of the attackers blown off their feet.

BLAM! The CANNON mounted at the cattle pen BLASTS the Romero men from the other side. Texian riflemen unloose a VOLLEY into the confused mass, which veers north.

EXT. ALAMO—PALISADE—NIGHT

Crockett and his men FIRE into the advancing Morales column, men falling left and right. The cannon FIRES, leveling Mexican soldiers, turning the column west toward the gate.

INT. BOWIE'S QUARTERS—NIGHT

Bowie awakens. Through his window we see the Morales column.

EXT. ALAMO—NIGHT

Jesus sprints, screaming without knowing it. A CANNON UNLOADS and half the men to the left are shredded by canister. He slams against the base of the wall with a dozen other survivors. Texians, including Travis, FIRE down into them.

EXT. ALAMO—DUQUE COLUMN

Colonel Duque's men, losing momentum, slow down fifty yards from the north wall.

COLONEL DUQUE (Spanish)
Halt! Ready—Aim—Fire!

The front row of his ragged lines aim through heavy smoke, the men behind aim between them.

COLONEL DUQUE (Spanish)
(cont'd)
Fire!

They unleash a VOLLEY at the north wall.

EXT. ALAMO—BASE OF NORTH WALL—NIGHT

Several of the men with Jesus are hit in the volley, BALLS RICOCHETING OFF the WALL by his head.

EXT. ALAMO—PALISADE—NIGHT

Crockett and his men FIRE at the Morales column soldiers as they run to the right, officers cursing and striking the men.

EXT. ALAMO—WEST WALL—NIGHT

General Cos's column charges the west wall. Included in his group are PIONEERS, broad axe-wielding soldiers wearing beards and bloody leather aprons.

With commands shouted by Bonham, the GUNNADE FIRES out through its hole in the wall but immediately a half-dozen soldiers, their backs against the wall, wheel and FIRE their MUSKETS into the hole.

EXT. ALAMO—OTHER SIDE OF WALL—HOLE—NIGHT

The two Texians operating the gun are blown back. The Pioneers begin to chop at the hole with an ax. Bonham gets off one more shot before he is riddled with bullets.

Above them, Texians expose themselves to get shots off. They fall under the massed MUSKET FIRE, leaving undefended gaps of several yards.

EXT. ALAMO—NORTH WALL PLATFORM—NIGHT

Ladders arrive and are pushed against the wall. Travis shouts orders as he stands on the north wall with his shotgun.

TRAVIS
Depress the cannon! Keep them off the walls!

Joe hands a loaded rifle to Travis, who moves to the edge, leans over and fires. The soldier next to Jesus falls. Jesus FIRES up over his head without aiming, panicked.

EXT. ALAMO—NORTH WALL—CONTINUOUS

Jesus' BALL hits Travis square in the forehead, knocking him back head-over-heels down the ramp.

He rolls to a stop at the feet of Joe.

Texians push ladders away from the edge with their rifle butts or FIRE down at the climbing Mexicans, but each time another ladder and another soldier takes its place.

Ward looks past the struggle just in front of him to a wave of charging reserves. He has a dozen men left.

WARD
Fall back!

As Ward turns to do so he is shot, killed.

EXT. A CONGRIEVE ROCKET POSITION OUTSIDE THE ALAMO

FLARES are loaded and fired, bursting in the air. Attached to parachutes, they spark red and white.

NOTE: This "fireworks" display will continue to the end of the final assault.

EXT. NORTH WALL—RAMP—NIGHT (CONTINUOUS)

Joe stares at lifeless Travis, looks around at the shouting, SHOOTING retreating defenders on the walls around him, then gently lays his shotgun down and backs, then walks, zombie-like toward Travis's quarters....

WE STAY WITH JOE as he walks through the courtyard—men running all around him, mayhem to which he's oblivious. Mexicans start to top the walls in twos and threes, then turn to run for the buildings in the courtyard.

INT. TRAVIS'S QUARTERS—NIGHT (CONTINUOUS)

Joe enters, looks around, walks to the back wall and sits. He spots Travis's saddlebag and holds it tight against his chest. He repeats over and over—

JOE
Soy negro, no disparo...

We push in on the saddlebag—the initials "WBT" prominent.

EXT. ALAMO CHURCH PLATFORM—NIGHT (CONTINUOUS)

Dickinson races down the ramp to—the Baptistry—where Susannah and the baby, along with other women, children, hide in the shadows.

DICKINSON
Susannah!...

They share a last look—and Dickinson returns to his post.

EXT. ALAMO—SOUTHWEST CORNER—NIGHT (CONTINUOUS)

Jameson sees the Mexicans behind them.

JAMESON
They're over the wall! Turn it around!

The crew struggles to turn the big cannon around.

AT THE PALISADE

Crockett hears, turns—hundreds of Mexican soldiers are streaming over the north wall now, coming down the ramps!

CROCKETT
Behind us!

The men turn and begin to FIRE almost without aiming into the throng of invaders, reloading frantically.

INT. LONG BARRACKS—NIGHT (CONTINUOUS)

The New Orleans Greys race into their fallback trenches.

EXT./INT. LONG BARRACKS—NIGHT (CONTINUOUS)

WE PULL BACK THROUGH ALL LONG BARRACKS ROOMS to see: A wave of soldados flooding into the smoke-filled rooms, SHOOTING, stabbing, screaming as the Texians fight back with knives, rifle butts, fists, teeth...

EXT. SW BATTERY—NIGHT (CONTINUOUS)

18-POUNDER, turned around now, FIRES—

EXT. LONG BARRACKS—NIGHT (CONTINUOUS)

The soldados are scattered by shrapnel from the cannon blast.

EXT. SW BATTERY—NIGHT (CONTINUOUS)

MUSKET FIRE cuts the Texian crew down from behind. Ladders appear on the wall and Soldados climb over, pushing the dead bodies of the Texians off the cannon and swinging it toward the chapel.

EXT. ALAMO—HIGH ANGLE SHOT—NIGHT (CONTINUOUS)

We see the whole layout FROM HIGH ABOVE, Mexicans streaming in over the north wall, over and through the west wall, up and over the lunette at the main gate, into the cattle pen...

EXT. ALAMO—PALISADE—NIGHT (CONTINUOUS)

Crockett and his men FIRE as they move sideways, making it behind the fortified breastworks in front of the church.

Tom Waters sets down the mutt dog and urges it to leave. Waters is shot and falls over. THREE TEXIANS near him jump the palisade and start to run. We follow one who makes it to the brush before he comes face to face with a charging LANCER. The Texian is run through.

INT. ALAMO—BAPTISTRY—NIGHT (CONTINUOUS)

Susanna Dickinson holds her baby tight, hiding in the darkness of a corner with Juana and the Esparzas.

EXT. ALAMO—PLATFORM—NIGHT (CONTINUOUS)

Bonham and Dickinson are riddled with GUNFIRE from every direction, Bonham tumbles down the ramp. Susannah, in the baptistry, sees her husband through the door and screams.

EXT. SOUTHWEST CORNER—18-POUNDER—NIGHT (CONTINUOUS)

KA-BOOM! The 18-POUNDER is FIRED down at the chapel entrance, blowing the thrown-together breastworks apart. Autry and several others are blown back, the rest ducking behind what's left of the barricade! Crockett kneels by Autry, who is dying. Crockett's arm is bleeding, shredded.

CROCKETT
Micajah—

MICAJAH AUTRY
They've killed me.

CROCKETT
I'm real sorry about all this.

Autry looks into his eyes, startled. He dies.

A CONCUSSION as another BLAST hits the remnants of the breastworks! Crockett and the others retreat into the church.

INT. ALAMO—BOWIE'S QUARTERS—NIGHT (CONTINUOUS)

Bowie, breathing hard, tenses as—a half-dozen Mexican soldiers rush into the room.

And are met with blasts from Bowie's pistols. Still they come and Bowie's eyes open in horror as the men ram their bay-

onets home, one with a musket stepping in close—FIRING. Bowie reaches for his knife but his lifeless hand instead finds a cameo of his beloved Ursula. It falls to the ground.

INT. ALAMO—CHURCH—NIGHT

Crockett's men, dead and alive, are all by the ramp—holding rifles, knives, and chunks of stone. Dug in for one last stand. They stare at the door which is draped in smoke, waiting for the inevitable.

The other SOUNDS FADE AWAY and we are left only with their RAGGED BREATHING. Crockett turns his head and sees, in the sacristy—Enrique Esparza. An odd moment between the famous man and the young, innocent boy. And then...

Fifty screaming Mexicans charge through the smoke, firing, thrusting bayonets. Crockett and his men are overwhelmed by a sea of bayonets. The chaos of the situation—so tight we can't really see much takes us to—

Black. And absolute silence. It's true you can't really hear it until it stops. And then we fade up on—

CU—SAM HOUSTON—ear to the ground. Hears nothing. He knows what we know. The Alamo has fallen.

EXT. GONZALES CAMP—DAY

Houston slowly rises, bearing the weight of all that is tragic about the situation. Then he looks up at—

THE SUN—bright hot in the sky. And then a VOLLEY BLAST and—

CU—A PAIR OF EYES OPEN AND SQUINT AT THE SUN.

EXT. COURTYARD—ALAMO—DAY

As we pull back we realize that the eyes belong to Crockett. He's on his knees, hands tied behind him, surrounded by his friends—all dead. His eyes lower and a gaze is leveled at—Santa Anna, dressed to the nines, a few feet away, staring at him. An EXECUTION SQUAD stands nearby, rifles pointed at Crockett. One of the riflemen is the *Battery Sergeant*, who looks nervous pointing his rifle at the legend. Nearby, Jesus watches from a crowd.

SANTA ANNA
Crockett! Davy Crockett!!

(Crockett just stares; Spanish)
If you wish to beg for your life, this would be the appropriate time.

(to Almonte, Spanish)
Explain this to him.

ALMONTE (English)
Throw yourself on the mercy of His Excellency Antonio López de Santa Anna!

CROCKETT
(smiles)
You're Santanna?

Santa Anna understands, nods.

CROCKETT (cont'd)
(to Almonte)
Thought he'd be taller.

Crockett, weary, looks around, sees generals, pioneers, horses, the squad of executioners. And then something else. One soldado is wearing Crockett's vest, another is holding his fiddle. Crockett lowers his head and chuckles at the absurdity of it all.

CROCKETT (cont'd)
(sotto)
Davy Crockett.

(back to Almonte)
Tell him I'm willing to discuss terms of surrender.

Almonte turns to Santa Anna, nods.

CROCKETT (cont'd)
If the General here will have his men put down their weapons and peacefully assemble, I will take you to General Houston and try my best to get him to spare most of your lives.

(Almonte is stunned)
That said, Sam's a might prickly so no promises.

(firm; right to Almonte)
Tell him.

Almonte tells Santa Anna, who bristles, and nods to the execution squad. Castrillón steps forward—

CASTRILLÓN (Spanish)
Excellency, please spare him!

SERGEANTO (Spanish)
Kill him!

The execution squad hesitates—a tad uneasy with their task. Crockett grins, stares right at the battery sergeant. Smiles.

CROCKETT
I'm a screamer....

SANTA ANNA (Spanish)
Kill him!

The men move forward to hack Crockett again and again with sabres.

HIGH AND WIDE

Crockett slumps over, dead. Hundreds of bodies litter the courtyard and the surrounding walls.

EXT. GONZALES CAMP—DAY

Houston watches as his growing army drills.

MOSELY BAKER
Fire by files—ready, aim, fire!

The soldiers aim and "fire" with unloaded muskets. Houston's eyes drift to the horizon, where a horse and rider approach.

On the horse is Susannah Dickinson holding her baby. And leading the horse—Joe.

EXT. GONZALES—TOWN—NIGHT

As the town burns behind them, wagon loads of civilians, crying, moaning with grief, leave their homes. Houston's army escorts them away.

Houston rides his horse alongside the wagons. He looks over, spots blind Mrs. Millsaps, crying in the back of a wagon.

We see Joe nearby watching. After a beat he disappears into the dark—in the opposite direction of the exodus.

A SWORD DRAWS A LINE IN THE SAND. We're in—

SANTA ANNA (Spanish) (V.O.)
Sabine river. The border with the United States.

EXT. BEXAR PLAZA—DAY

Beneath the San Fernando Church, Santa Anna is mapping out a strategy in the dirt.

SANTA ANNA (Spanish)
Houston is running for help. We must move quickly to cut him off.

(marks with his sword)
Bexar. Fannin, here in Goliad—must not be allowed to join Houston. Colonel Morales, you will take a thousand soldiers and sweep south.

(another line)
General Gaona, you will take 800 troops and sweep north.

(another line)
General Ramirez y Sesma you will march straight through Texas. I will attend to matters here, then join you with 700 men. We leave the women here and we carry only bedrolls and weapons.

CASTRILLÓN (Spanish)
Your Excellency, is it wise for you to be separated from the other forces?

SANTA ANNA (Spanish))
This war is over.

(sticks his sword in ground)
It is time to finish our task.

EXT. TEXAS—PLAINS—DAY

The Texian army moves eastward, accompanied by more and more settlers. Houston, alone with his thoughts, is aware of the looks he's getting from the settlers forced to leave their homes.

VARIOUS SHOTS

The caravan—soldiers and settlers moves east.

EXT. COLORADO RIVER—DAY

The Texian army, with settlers in tow, crosses the river.

ON THE BANK

Seguin and his Tejanos pass Houston, who stands on his horse, watching. Seguin pulls alongside.

SEGUIN
We had more deserters last night.

(hard to say)
Some of the men...

(off Houston's look)
They think we're headed for the border.

HOUSTON
I hope Santa Anna shares their concerns.

(off Seguin's confusion)
We camp here, wait for Fannin to join us.

Houston rides away, leaving Seguin to ponder.

EXT. TEXIAN ARMY CAMP—DUSK

Rain pours down on the camp. A RIDER approaches, dismounts. Several Texians come to greet him.

RIDER
They're all dead—Goliad—executed! Fannin and 400 men.

The word spreads—MUMBLINGS, MOANS, SHOUTS

Houston opens his tent, looks out at the Rider, who walks over. We don't hear what is said, but Houston's face drops a bit and he retreats into his tent.

The men outside stare at the closed tent with derision.

EXT. COLORADO RIVER—DAY

Bushes part and we GET A GLIMPSE of the Mexican Army across the river. Deaf Smith runs back toward camp.

EXT. CAMP—DAY

Men load weapons, prepare themselves for a fight.

J.C. NEILL
I heard they marched those men right outta Goliad, shot 'em in the back.

MOSELY BAKER
It's time, boys.

HOUSTON (O.S.)
Break camp. We continue east!

They all look up to see Houston standing nearby.

MOSELY BAKER
General Sesma and a good portion of the Mexican army is right across the river. And we're running?! Alamo, Goliad! They gotta pay! If not now, when?!

HOUSTON
Break camp!

Houston walks away, leaving Seguin and Baker to stare at one another.

INT. HOUSTON'S TENT—DAY

Houston packs. Seguin enters, dumbfounded.

SEGUIN
They are ready to fight, General.

Houston ignores Seguin, keeps packing.

SEGUIN (cont'd)
Sam!

HOUSTON
No.

SEGUIN
Why not?

HOUSTON
Because none of it means anything without Santa Anna.

SEGUIN
If you do not fight Ramirez y Sesma now I am afraid we will not have an army to fight Santa Anna.

HOUSTON
This army, this infamous army, has ONE battle in them. Maybe. I'd prefer it to count.

Seguin takes this in, moves to leave.

HOUSTON (cont'd)
Juan...

(Seguin turns)
Don't question me again.

EXT. ROAD—DAY

We see personal belongings—trunks, clothes, carts, even a piano dumped in the mud alongside the road as a LARGE GROUP OF SETTLERS joins the exodus. A Settler slides in next to Mosley Baker.

SETTLER
How far east we gotta run to be safe? As long as you keep retreating, we have to, too. Gimme one good reason why you don't just dig in here and fight.

Baker nods toward Houston, who rides alongside the teamsters.

MOSLEY BAKER
Ain't a good one, but...

Houston rides his white horse Saracen alongside a newcomer's wagon, his eyes fixed on—

AN OLD-TIMER in the wagon. With a bottle.

HOUSTON
Where you coming from?

OLD TIMER
San Felipe.

The Old Timer raises a bottle, takes a pull, sees Houston eyeing him and holds the bottle out, offering.

Houston absently licks his lips—his face says he'd love a drink himself. Then his eyes go to the other people in the wagon—a little boy and woman we've seen before. Houston locks eyes with the little boy. After a beat...

CHARLIE
Your horse is the biggest.

HOUSTON
What's your name, son?

CHARLIE
Charlie.

MRS. AYERS
Tell him your last name, Charlie.

CHARLIE
Travis.

Houston makes the connection, shares a look with Mrs. Ayers, who glares. Houston's horse slows as the cart moves ahead, little Charlie staring back at a tortured Houston.

EXT. SWAMPY LAND—DAY
Santa Anna's troops slog through the mud.

JESUS (Spanish)
What kind of place is this?

A cannon is stuck. Men (with Jesus) try to free it with Oxen.

SANTA ANNA (Spanish)
Leave it! Move!

CASTRILLÓN (Spanish)
General, that is the fifth cannon we've discarded.

SANTA ANNA (Spanish)
(paying no heed)
We have a good moon tonight—we will make use of the light and keep moving.

EXT. FARM—DAY
The Texians start setting up tents. Houston pulls the saddle off his horse, sees someone coming—riding slowly.

HOUSTON
Shite.

T.J. Rusk, looking more polished than the ragged Texians.

RUSK (V.O.)
"Sir, the enemy are laughing you to scorn. You must fight them."

EXT. A CLEARING—DAY
Rusk reads from a letter. Houston tosses rocks.

RUSK
"You must retreat no further. The country expects you to fight. The salvation of the country depends on your doing so." Signed David G. Burnet, President.

Rusk folds the letter, offers it to Houston, who ignores him.

HOUSTON
Where is the pig thief these days—Harrisburg?

RUSK
President Burnet as well as the rest of the provisional government have abandoned Harrisburg.

HOUSTON
(walks away)
Seems they're retreating faster than I am.

RUSK
Sir, I have been given authority to replace you! General?!...

ANOTHER PART OF THE WOODS
Seguin walks up behind Houston...

SEGUIN
General... Sam! Talk with him. Share your strategy.
(off Houston's look)
Have you a strategy?

HOUSTON
A general who has to cajole soldiers into following is no general. I'm not fond of war councils. Fannin was fond of war councils.

SEGUIN
These men, they believe you're a coward!

Houston takes this without a flinch. After a beat...

HOUSTON
Did you know I told Crockett to come to Texas? And the others, now dead, at their posts by my orders...

SEGUIN
You warned them not to fort up.

HOUSTON
In these times it is very difficult to maintain your honor without losing your life. But can a man choose honor, and death, for another?

(after a beat)
They weren't good men, Juan.... But damn they were good men.

INT. HOUSTON'S TENT—NIGHT
Houston sits, waiting for—Rusk, who enters with Seguin....

RUSK
General.

Houston waits until Rusk takes a seat. Then he speaks, quietly, efficiently, eyes down, hardly looking at Rusk.

HOUSTON
Twenty odd years ago. Napoleon returns from exile in Elba, puts together an army and moves east. Swiftly—trying to gain power before an alliance between nations can occur. Wellington, with fewer men, fewer armaments, stays one step ahead of the French—teasing them with his presence—knowing that a large army will splinter in order to keep up. He moves and he waits, moves and waits.... for Napoleon to make a mistake—to fall into a scenario that condemns him to defeat. Wellington chooses the setting for victory before it exists for him, before he lays eyes on it. It has an open battleground, a sloping plane, cover for encampment and an opportunity to surprise the enemy flank.

Rusk listens, wondering what the hell this has to do with—and then Houston raises his eyes, fixing on Rusk.

HOUSTON (cont'd)
The Mexican army is splintered and though they don't know it, Santa Anna's troops subsist on gasps of air and sips of hope. I share Wellington's battleground vision, though I know not the name of the place I imagine. I, sir, do not consider myself Wellington. Santa Anna, however, does consider himself the Napoleon of the West. We shall move and wait until he makes a mistake and presents us with his Waterloo.

Rusk considers this, then after a moment, rises.

RUSK
Thank you, General.

(stops, turns)
General, might I enlist as a private in your army?

EXT. TEXIAN CAMP—DAY

A Mexican soldier is dragged into camp—
he's been beaten badly. Seguin inter-
cedes, props the soldier by a tree, kneels
to talk to him.

EXT. OUTSIDE TEXIAN CAMP—DAY

Soldiers wave good-bye to their families
as the civilian exodus moves on. Houston
looks over two six-pound cannons.

J.C. NEILL
A gift from the citizens of Cincin-
nati.

HOUSTON
I shall have to send them my
regards.

Seguin, with Neill and Deaf Smith, races
over with a saddlebag.

J.C. NEILL
Deaf captured a Mexican courier.

SEGUIN
His letters tell us Santa Anna is
nearby ... *and separated from the
rest of his army.*

Seguin hands over the saddlebag.

SEGUIN *(cont'd)*
The courier had this bag.

"WBT" stenciled on it. Houston's face
turns hard.

EXT. SAN JACINTO—DAY

Mexican troops, dead tired, set up camp
at the edge of the woods. Santa Anna,
with Almonte, walks by inspecting and
looking out onto the field in front of
him—half mile long, gently sloping up
and away, with a stand of trees to one
side. Castrillón strides up...

CASTRILLÓN (Spanish)
General, we have reports of
troop movement. Houston's army
is less than three miles away.

SANTA ANNA (Spanish)
(excited)
We will break camp and chase
the coward.

CASTRILLÓN (Spanish)
Sir,... he's not moving. He is on
his way *here.*

(points to far woods)
His scouts were spotted in those
woods. *Behind us.* We are cut off
from all our armies except Cos.

Santa Anna considers this, scratches his
neck.

SANTA ANNA (Spanish)
How many men?

CASTRILLÓN (Spanish)
Perhaps as many as 700.
(off Santa Anna's look)
We are at a disadvantage. Our
backs are against a body of water
with only a small bridge for
retreat.

SANTA ANNA (Spanish)
With General Cos's men we will
double Houston's army.

CASTRILLÓN (Spanish)
Cos won't be here until tomorrow.

ALMONTE (Spanish)
We should prepare breastworks
and put the men on alert. We are
only vulnerable tonight.

SANTA ANNA (Spanish)
Houston has water at his back as
well. Two cannon shots and he
will run like a rabbit.

EXT. TEXIAN CAMP—DAY

The Texians dismount and start to start
unloading. Houston walks past the men,
strides through a copse of trees and—

Right out into the open field. From where
he stands he can see the Mexican camp—
troops rapidly preparing breastworks
consisting of trunks, wagons, anything
that provides a wall.

Houston takes a pinch of snuff (or is it
opium?) and closes his eyes—like he's
soaking it in, or reliving a dream. And it
seems dreamlike to us, too, for around
him THE WIND SWIRLS, blowing his
hair.

HOUSTON (V.O.)
"Wellington chooses the setting
for victory before it exists for
him, before he lays eyes on it. It
has an open battleground, a sloping plane, cover for encampment
and an opportunity to surprise
the enemy flank."

*We see each of these things laid out before
us...* Houston opens his eyes.

HOUSTON *(cont'd)*
(to the field)
Do you have a name?... What do
they call you?...

EXT. TEXIAN CAMP—DAY

The army, fully aware of the proximity of
the enemy, is hard at work, preparing to
fight.

Houston reaches up, touches a leaf, grips
it between his thumb and forefinger.
Seguin watches.

HOUSTON
Damp. We have to keep our
powder dry.

Houston walks away, into his tent.
Seguin just watches. Mosely Baker and
Rusk walk over.

MOSELY BAKER
Well?...

Seguin just shakes his head.

MOSELY BAKER *(cont'd)*
He don't make up his mind soon,
we'll fight without him.

EXT. MEXICAN ARMY CAMP—NIGHT

All along the now complete breastworks,
soldiers are on their guard—waiting,
watching for the attack they feel will
come. Behind the men—Castrillón standing, watching.

EXT. TEXIAN CAMP—NIGHT

Seguin's men, a Tejano group, sleep. But
Seguin is awake, staring into the night.

INT. HOUSTON'S TENT—NIGHT

Houston stares at an oil lamp. A MOTH
circles it, lands on the glass, drawn to the
light. AS WE MOVE IN ON IT...

A FLARE OF SUNLIGHT presents to us—

EXT. BATTLEFIELD—DAWN

Empty, pristine.

EXT. MEXICAN CAMP—DAY

Up all night, the Mexican soldiers are
almost nodding off when they hear
BUGLES. They turn and see—

GENERAL COS and his army approaching
camp. Cos's weary men flop down with
their packs and start to fall asleep immediately.

ALMONTE (Spanish)
We are safe now.

Castrillón, not sure, just looks at Almonte.

ALMONTE (Spanish)
(cont'd)
(an order)
Rest, men. Rest for battle.

EXT. TEXIAN CAMP—DAY

Houston, too, hears the bugles. He's standing with Seguin, watching as Cos's army reaches camp.

HOUSTON
How many?

SEGUIN
Six hundred troops. Altogether, thirteen or fourteen hundred.

Houston considers, Seguin watches, waits—moment of truth.

HOUSTON
There is a bridge behind the Mexican army.
(off Seguin's look)
Send Deaf Smith and his boys to burn it.

Seguin perks up, starts to leave...

HOUSTON (cont'd)
Do we have music?

SEGUIN
A drummer, I believe.

HOUSTON
See if you can find him a friend or two.

Seguin grins, nods and races off.

EXT. TEXIAN CAMP—DAY

The Texians are preparing to fight, loading rifles. Houston finds Seguin, also preparing.

HOUSTON
Captain Seguin, you and your men will guard the camp.
(off Juan's look)
There could be confusion out there; men shooting any Mexican they see.

SEGUIN
General, Sir, you ordered me to stay; I stayed. My friends are also dead.... This is our fight, too. Even more than yours.

HOUSTON
(after a beat)
You'll join Sherman on the left flank.

EXT. MEXICAN CAMP—DAY

The Mexicans are sleeping, relaxing.

EXT. TEXIAN CAMP—DAY

Texians, antsy, ready: Various shots:

•• Seguin and his men put white cards in their hats so as not to be confused with the enemy.

•• Mathew sections off his powder, his hand shakes as he works.

•• The DRUMMER gets ready, tapping his sticks. TWO FIFERS sit under a nearby tree, warming up.

DRUMMER
(suddenly concerned)
What do we play?

The Fifers share a look—good question.

FIFER
I dunno... we never attacked anybody before.
(after a beat)
I mostly only know bawdy love songs.

DRUMMER
"Come to the Bower?"

FIFER
Know that.

Houston emerges from his tent, looks at the men. They rise, ready. He walks along, looking at them, sizing them up.

HOUSTON
You will remember this battle, remember each minute of it, each second... until the day you die.

His horse is delivered. Houston mounts as they all watch.

HOUSTON (cont'd)
But that is for tomorrow, gentlemen—for today remember Goliad. Remember the Alamo. The hour is at hand.

He rides forward and the men start to line up and move through the brush to—

EXT. BATTLEFIELD—DAY

Houston exits the brush and is joined by several cavalrymen. Houston turns to a handsome, good-to-go CALVARYMAN.

HOUSTON
Lamar, correct?

CAVALRYMAN
Yessir, Mirabeau B. Lamar.

HOUSTON
What does the B stand for?

LAMAR
Bonaparte, Sir.

HOUSTON
(almost laughs)
You, Sir, will ride to my right.

LAMAR
With all due respect, Sir, we prefer to be at the front.

HOUSTON
And you shall.

Houston moves front and center as the Texians infantry emerges from the woods—two deep and wide across. Mathew is in the middle—barely able to breath.

The two cannons are turned toward the Mexicans. Houston looks to the Drummer, who, after a beat of "who me" plays "Come to the Bower," joined by the two fife players.

Houston raises one hand, holds it in the air for a few seconds, then lowers it and—THE CANNONS FIRE

ON THE MEXICAN LINE

Things go flying, as the Mexican soldiers, awakened, start to scurry about, grab muskets. General confusion.

TEXIAN LINE

HOUSTON
Forward!

The Texians start walking forward. There is a POPPING of musket fire from the Mexicans, balls riffling through the grass around them. The men walk closer, closer—

HOUSTON (cont'd)
Volley formation!!

The front row of men stop and aim, the men behind aiming over their shoulders—

HOUSTON (cont'd)
Fire!

A VOLLEY rips into the few Mexican defenders who peek over the barricade to fire.

HOUSTON (cont'd)
Resume advance!

Mathew gets up from his knee, nervously reloads as he walks.

Houston looks down the line of troops, one or two falling from musket fire. He raises his hand again and—

The cannons fire into the Mexicans, blowing up a barricade.

MEXICAN CAMP

Santa Anna emerges from his tent, not fully dressed—sees the chaos around him. Castrillón organizes his men in the middle of the breastworks and orders them to fire.

ON THE LEFT FLANK

Seguin, Sherman, and two dozen men on horseback move stealthily behind and through a stand of trees.

TEXIAN LINE

> HOUSTON
> Volley formation.
> (front row kneels)
> Fire!
> (they fire)
> Resume advance!

The men are antsy as they move forward. When two other men drop from musket fire a quickened step turns into a trot—

> BAKER
> Remember the Alamo!

> TEXIANS
> Remember Goliad!

The ranks break and the Texians race for the Mexican lines.

> HOUSTON
> Form ranks! Form ranks!

But the men aren't listening. Houston spurs his horse forward into battle.

MEXICAN SIDE

Castrillón is also trying to hold ranks.

> CASTRILLÓN (Spanish)
> Hold ranks, hold ranks!

And then Castrillón sees something—

Seguin and his men racing in from the flank, firing, breaking any chance the Mexicans have of holding. Castrillón's men start to retreat into the chaos.

> BATRES (Spanish)
> General, we must pull back.

> CASTRILLÓN (Spanish)
> Forty battles and I've never shown my back. I am too old to do it now.

Castrillón turns to see Santa Anna shout orders that no one hears. He spots Castrillón, they share a look, then Santa Anna grabs an errant horse, mounts and joins the retreat.

Castrillón turns back to the battle just as—

The Texians make it to the breastworks and brutal fighting ensues with the few Mexicans who have stayed to fight.

Castrillón folds his arms and stands staring at the charge and then is overwhelmed with shot as the Texians hop over the breastworks.

Houston wheels on his horse, and is shot in the ankle. He and the horse tumble. Houston gets up, limping, accepts another horse from a Calvaryman and mounts.

IN THE WOODS

Mexicans run for their lives as Texians give chase—firing, stabbing, shouting, "Remember the Alamo!"

One of the Texians is Mathew, flush with adrenaline, he finds himself alone in the woods, moving forward. Then he hears something, freezes and—

Jesus jumps out—they both freeze for a moment. Two boys. They almost share a smile and then... They both discharge their rifles, wounding one another... And fall to the ground.

PEGGY'S LAKE

The Mexicans arrive at the lake, realize they are trapped, throw down their muskets and start wading, jumping into the water. The Texians follow them right in—stabbing, firing, fighting with bloodlust. Houston appears on horseback.

> HOUSTON
> Pull back! Pull back! Damn your manners, men!

Batres is shot in the back. His horrified face lands in the water, looking right at us. As the air bubbles from his lungs and his blood fills the frame—

EXT. TEXIAN CAMP—LATER—DAY

The battle is over. Houston sits under an oak tree, being treated by a DOCTOR. He goes to his snuff box and takes a pinch to kill the pain.

A group of MEXICAN prisoners sit together, guarded by Rusk and others. Almonte is among them.

A string of new prisoners, haggard, bloody, defeated, tied together by rope, are led into camp by Deaf Smith. One of the prisoners, in a private's uniform, hangs his head, trying not to be recognized. The sitting prisoners take note—

> SITTING PRISONER (Spanish)
> He lives! El Presidente lives! Viva Santa Anna!

Deaf Smith and other Texians turn and stare at the private. When he lifts his head we see it is Santa Anna.

> ALMONTE (V.O.)
> The General wants you to know that the man who conquers the Napoleon of the West is born to no common destiny.

EXT. UNDER THE TREE—LATER—DAY

Santa Anna sits on a box with Almonte nearby to translate. A group of Texians, thirsting for blood, eye the proceedings.

> ALMONTE
> And now it remains for him to be generous to the vanquished.

> HOUSTON
> You should have remembered that at the Alamo.

Santa Anna and Almonte realize the delicacy of the situation.

> ALMONTE
> His Excellency is willing to discuss terms of surrender.

> MOSELY BAKER
> I say we hang him from this very tree!

A popular idea. Houston stares hard at Santa Anna, who, feeling the tension, whispers something to Almonte.

> ALMONTE
> The General would also like to humbly remind that he, like you, General, is a Mason.

Houston waits a beat more, then slowly nods, takes another hit from the snuff box. Santa Anna watches...

> SANTA ANNA
> Por favor?...

ALMONTE
He wonders if you might share a bit of your opium? For the nerves?

MOSELY BAKER
To hell with his nerves. Let's kill him and be done with it.

HOUSTON
No. You'll settle for blood.

(to Santa Anna)
I want Texas.

Houston hands over the opium tin.

EXT. FIELD/WOODS—DUSK
Seguin slowly walks through the field. Then he stops, drops to both knees, and looks around at the bodies of Mexican soldiers lying all around him. Questioning everything.

AS WE MOVE PAST SEVERAL BODIES WE FIND Mathew and Jesus lying where we last saw them, slowly dying, breathing with difficulty, too hurt to move. They are looking at each other with

slightly glazed eyes. Mathew finally speaks, softly—

MATHEW (Spanish)
Where you come from, friend?...

Jesus looks around weakly—

JESUS (Spanish)
From here. I am a Tejano.

(English; explaining)
From Texas.

MATHEW (English)
Yeah... me, too.

They stare at one another until the life leaves their eyes.

EXT. HILLS OUTSIDE BEXAR—DAY

Seguin brings his horse to a stop. He stares at something. A SHEPHERD stands nearby, looks up at Seguin...

SHEPHERD
Senor Seguin... you have returned.

SEGUIN
A man should keep his word.

And then we see what Seguin was staring at—THE ALAMO—in the distance below. Seguin starts forward on his horse and as he heads down the hill, we—FADE TO BLACK.

Santa Anna was spared and Texas was won.

Houston was plagued until his death by those who blamed him for not going to the defense of the Alamo.

Juan Seguin kept his promise to return to the Alamo. He buried the bones and ashes of his fellow Tejano and Texian defenders in Bexar, where they rest today.

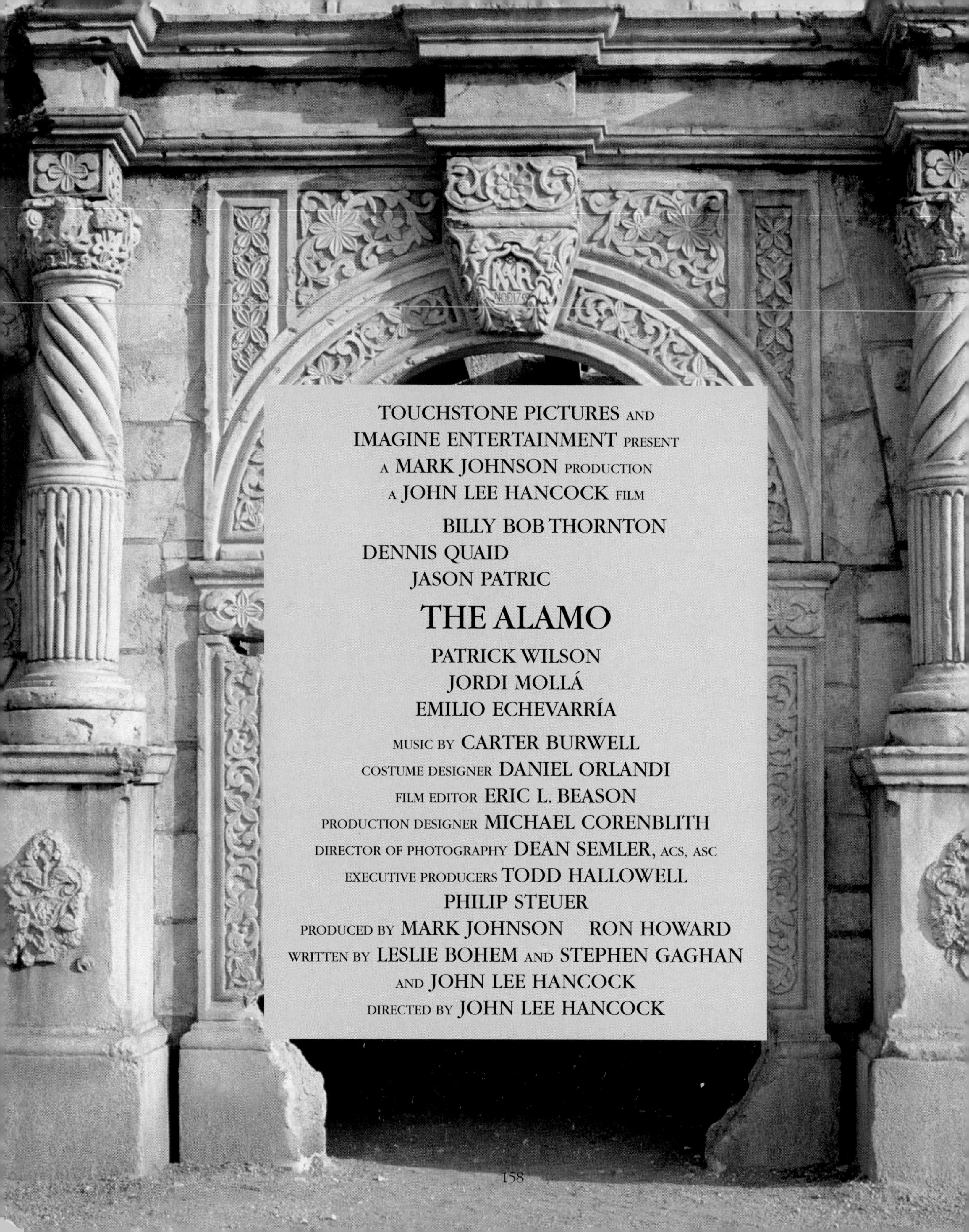

TOUCHSTONE PICTURES AND
IMAGINE ENTERTAINMENT PRESENT
A MARK JOHNSON PRODUCTION
A JOHN LEE HANCOCK FILM

BILLY BOB THORNTON
DENNIS QUAID
JASON PATRIC

THE ALAMO

PATRICK WILSON
JORDI MOLLÁ
EMILIO ECHEVARRÍA

MUSIC BY CARTER BURWELL
COSTUME DESIGNER DANIEL ORLANDI
FILM EDITOR ERIC L. BEASON
PRODUCTION DESIGNER MICHAEL CORENBLITH
DIRECTOR OF PHOTOGRAPHY DEAN SEMLER, ACS, ASC
EXECUTIVE PRODUCERS TODD HALLOWELL
PHILIP STEUER
PRODUCED BY MARK JOHNSON   RON HOWARD
WRITTEN BY LESLIE BOHEM AND STEPHEN GAGHAN
AND JOHN LEE HANCOCK
DIRECTED BY JOHN LEE HANCOCK

A SELECTED ALAMO BIBLIOGRAPHY

Davis, William C., *Three Roads to the Alamo* (1998, New York: Harper Collins)

Edmondson, J. R., *The Alamo Story: From Early History to Recent Conflicts* (2000, Plano: Republic of Texas Press)

Groneman, Bill, *Defense of a Legend: Crockett and the de la Peña Diary* (1994, Plano: Republic of Texas Press)

Groneman, Bill, *Eyewitness to the Alamo* (1996, Plano: Republic of Texas Press)

Hardin, Stephen L., Texian Iliad: *A Military History of the Texas Revolution*, 1835-1836 (1994, Austin: University of Texas Press)

Hardin, Stephen L., *The Alamo 1836: Santa Anna's Texas Campaign* (2001, Oxford: Osprey Publishing)

Huffines, Alan C., *Blood of Noble Men: The Alamo Siege and Battle—An Illustrated Chronology* (1999, Austin: Eakin Press) Illustrated by Gary S. Zaboly.

Jackson, Jack, *The Alamo: An Epic told From Both Sides* (2002, Austin: Paisano Graphics)

Kilgore, Dan, *How Did Davy Die?* (1978, College Station: Texas A&M Press)

Lindley, Thomas Ricks, *Alamo Traces* (2003, Plano: Republic of Texas Press)

Long, Jeff, *Duel of Eagles* (1990, New York: William Morrow & Co.) History

Lord, Walter, *A Time to Stand* (1961, New York: Harper & Brothers)

Peña, José Enrique de la (Translated and edited by Carmen Perry, Introduction by James E. Crisp) *With Santa Anna in Texas: A Personal Narrative of the Revolution* (Expanded Edition, 1997, College Station: Texas A&M Press)

Nelson, George, *The Alamo: An Illustrated History* (1998, Dry Frio Canyon Texas: Aldine Press)

Thompson, Frank, *Alamo Movies* (1991, East Berlin, Pennsylvania: Old Mill Books)

Thompson, Frank, *The Alamo: A Cultural History* (2001, Dallas: Taylor Publishing Co.)

Thompson, Frank, *The Alamo* (2002, San Diego: Thunder Bay)

Tinkle, Lon, *Thirteen Days to Glory: The Siege of the Alamo* (1958, New York: McGraw-Hill Book Co.)

Todish, Tim J. and Terry S. Todish, *The Alamo Sourcebook* 1836 (1998, Austin: Eakin Press)

ACKNOWLEDGMENTS

Many "making of" books are just product, beautifully produced volumes designed to help publicize the motion picture in question. I certainly hope this one fulfills its commercial requirements—and it certainly is beautiful—but to me *The Alamo* is more than that—it's a labor of love.

I have held a deep interest in the battle of the Alamo—and the films made about it—since my earliest childhood. It has been one of the great pleasures and privileges of my life to be involved in this film in even the most peripheral way, and I am deeply grateful to everyone who welcomed me to the set and who helped me through the long, rather rocky, process of getting this book off the ground.

First I want to thank John Lee Hancock and Michael Corenblith. Both of them are supremely talented, incredibly generous, and genuinely nice guys. And if you think such a combination is common, you've never been to Hollywood.

And while we're on the subject of nice guys, a big thank you goes to Ron Howard and Todd Hallowell for bringing me into this project to begin with. That original summit meeting at the Omni in Austin in April 2002 was one of the most enjoyable experiences in my Alamo life and I appreciate being among those invited. Speaking of which, I also want to thank my fellow panel members, and pals, Steve Hardin, Alan Huffines, Steve Harrigan, Jim Crisp, Bruce Winders, Frank de la Teja, and Andres Tijerina.

On the set of *The Alamo* I was always made welcome and comfortable by the great Katie R. Kelly, as well as by Mark Johnson, Phil Steuer, and publicist extraordinaire Ernie Malik. I owe a special debt of thanks to Ernie, in fact, for all the material he provided for this book.

During my several visits to Texas to either work on this book or appear in my scenes as an extra (keep your eyes peeled), I imposed upon the hospitality of Joan and Marcus Headley in San Antonio and Annie, Callan, Jill, and Nick Newton in Austin. They're all great friends of mine; the best way to tell which house I'm in is whether I'm sleeping in the Davy Crockett Room or the Winnie the Pooh Room.

My gratitude also goes to Alan Adolphsen and Glen Adolphsen of Adolphsen Bros., Craig Barron, Krystyna Barron and Kane Brassington of Matte World Digital, Shannon Berning, Christine Cadena, Holly Clark, Craig Covner, Richard Curilla, Deborah Daly, Frank DeMaio, Howard Green, Larry Grimsley, Keith Hollaman, Paul Andrew Hutton, Ned Huthmacher, Susann Jones, Jerry Laing, Tony Malanowski, Esther Margolis, Nick Medrano, Daniel Orlandi, Tracey Ramos, Eugene Reimers, John Sabel, Dean Semler, Paul Sugarman, Tammy Troglin, Billy Bob Thornton, Chuck Tressler of Cannons Online, Inc., Martha Utterback, DRT Library at the Alamo, and Gary Zaboly.

And, most important of all, my deepest thanks go to the wonderful, the miraculous Claire McCulloch Thompson, recently voted by a panel of experts as Greatest Wife Ever.

ABOUT THE AUTHOR

Frank Thompson is a writer, filmmaker, and film historian, the author of over thirty books, including five on the Alamo. He lives in North Hollywood, California with his wife, Claire.